"COLD?" LUCAS ASKED, HIS HANDS ON THE sleigh's reins.

"A little," Corrie murmured.

"That's part of the fun. To counteract it, you have to dress warmly, bring along a heated brick for your feet, and cuddle close to the driver."

Corrie sent a quelling look in his direction and deliberately moved a few inches away. He chuckled and urged the horse to go faster.

Before long, even though she was thoroughly chilled, Corrie realized she was enjoying herself. She was almost sorry to see the hotel appear ahead of them. That meant the end of the ride was in sight. "Breathtaking," she said softly as the facade of the great building was lit by the setting sun. Then Corrie blinked. Surely she was imagining that in one high window she'd seen a curtain twitch.

She stared at it, mesmerized, until she began to feel light-headed. Reality faded away, followed by an overwhelming need. Corrie turned in the seat, lifting her hands to frame Lucas's startled face. She forced his head down until his lips met hers, savoring the first brief contact, then returning to linger.

She lost herself in the deeper kiss that followed. She'd kissed men before, but never had it been so intense. Never had it felt so right.

"Mmmm," Lucas moaned. Corrie suddenly became aware of what she was doing, and pulled away. What on earth had gotten into her?

WHAT ARE *LOVESWEPT* ROMANCES?

They are stories of true romance and touching emotion. We believe those two very important ingredients are constants in our highly sensual and very believable stories in the LOVE-SWEPT line. Our goal is to give you, the reader, stories of consistently high quality that may sometimes make you laugh, sometimes make you cry, but are always fresh and creative and contain many delightful surprises within their pages.

Most romance fans read an enormous number of books. Those they truly love, they keep. Others may be traded with friends and soon forgotten. We hope that each LOVESWEPT romance will be a treasure—a "keeper." We will always try to publish

LOVE STORIES YOU'LL NEVER FORGET
BY AUTHORS YOU'LL ALWAYS REMEMBER

The Editors

RELATIVE
STRANGERS

KATHY LYNN
EMERSON

BANTAM BOOKS

NEW YORK · TORONTO · LONDON · SYDNEY · AUCKLAND

RELATIVE STRANGERS

A Bantam Book / November 1997

ISBN 0-553-44584-7

Published simultaneously in the United States and Canada

*Bantam Books are published by Bantam Books, a division of Bantam Dou-
bleday Dell Publishing Group, Inc. Its trademark, consisting of the words
"Bantam Books" and the portrayal of a rooster, is Registered in U.S. Patent
and Trademark Office and in other countries. Marca Registrada. Bantam
Books, 1540 Broadway, New York, New York 10036.*

PRINTED IN THE UNITED STATES OF AMERICA

OPM   10 9 8 7 6 5 4 3 2 1

This one is for
Elaine Emerson Smith,
with belated apologies for running
away that one Christmas
(but it did give me the idea for
the book)

ONE

"Shopping for a Christmas present, Corrie?" Rachel gave her friend a nudge and a saucy wink.

Caught staring at the good-looking stranger, Corrie Ballantyne sent Rachel a rueful glance. "Dream on."

"He's a dream boat, all right. Tall. Dark. Handsome." Rachel began to hum "Some Enchanted Evening" under her breath.

In spite of her best intentions, Corrie's gaze slid back across the room crowded with hotel guests and townspeople. She wasn't looking for a vacation romance. On the other hand, there seemed to be no harm in fantasizing a bit.

This particular man could provoke lustful thoughts in a nearsighted octogenarian. That thick, wavy black hair was just meant to be mussed. His narrow face featured high cheekbones, a long, straight nose, and a strong jaw. In combination with height and a superb physique, those assets produced the perfect image of a handsome, mysterious, slightly dangerous heart-breaker.

The outfit he wore reinforced the image. He was in costume, decked out in all the sartorial splendor of a proper gentleman of the late 1880s. The entire staff of the Sinclair House was in nineteenth-century attire, since the evening's entertainment at the hotel was billed as "an old-fashioned Christmas Eve," but he alone managed to project the illusion of a Gothic hero.

The Currier & Ives setting was nice, but to Corrie's mind this dash of Victorian melodrama added just the right touch. She continued to stare, envisioning him as an English aristocrat with some deep, dark secret sorrow. She was quite pleased with that interpretation until he bent down to speak to a man in a wheelchair.

He smiled then, a real dazzler that revealed an unexpected dimple in his formidable chin. The image of brooding misanthrope vanished. Only a gorgeous specimen of the male of the species remained.

"Glad I suggested we come here?" Rachel asked.

"Here" was an opulent hotel left over from the nineteenth century. One of the few summer resorts to survive that bygone era, in part by winterizing one section of the hotel, it was now exclusive, expensive, and unique, catering to those who were fed up with nothing but fast food and generic motels. There weren't even any television sets in the bedrooms. Instead, guests had to leave their spacious, handsomely appointed chambers and seek out the variety of live entertainment offered in parlors, private dining halls, ballrooms, and lounges. In this aptly named Fireside Room, fragrant applewood burned in a huge granite fireplace, its pungent aroma blending with the scent of pine needles.

Corrie shifted her attention to Rachel, though she remained aware of the man across the room. "This place makes me remember the stories my grand-mother used to tell my brothers and me when we were kids. All about the big hotels in the Catskills, and about my great-grandmother Daisy."

"Was she the one who was scrubbing pots and pans in the hotel kitchen, wearing her fingers to the bone, when your great-grandfather came along, possibly on a big white horse, to rescue her?"

"That's the one. She married him and scrubbed his pots and pans instead." Corrie knew she sounded cyni-cal, but the role of the woman in marriage had been a sore point with her since her own mother's death just after Christmas the year before.

Her subsequent estrangement from her father and brothers was the reason she was here in Maine for the holidays, rather than back home in New York State. No way would she take on the traditional woman's role with her family, not after her mother had sacri-ficed her health by catering to the menfolk.

Corrie Ballantyne had no intention of letting his-tory repeat itself.

Deciding it was time to focus on something else, since there was no sense in dwelling on a past she couldn't change, Corrie searched the crowd for Mr.

Tall, Dark, and Handsome. He would make a fine diversion.

Just as she spotted him, he looked up, staring right at her with a mixture of interest and what seemed to be irritation. After a long, breathless moment, he broke eye contact.

"Well," Corrie murmured. "That was odd." And strangely erotic.

She was relieved when a touch on her forearm and a pleasantly modulated female voice distracted her from her increasingly unrealistic thoughts about the stranger.

"We're all going to sing Christmas carols soon. I hope you'll join us." The woman who'd checked them into the hotel earlier that day had a hostess's smile firmly fixed on her plain, winter-pale face. "I'm Joyce Sinclair," she added.

"Sinclair, you say?" Rachel pounced on the surname. "Does that mean you own this place?"

"The family does." Joyce absently patted one of the elaborate twists into which her brown hair, liberally streaked with white strands, had been styled.

She was, Corrie speculated, one of those women who always looked years younger than they really were. Not a bit of makeup aided that youthful appearance, either. The lack of any lent a certain authenticity to her turn-of-the-century costume, an elaborate gown of deep wine-red with flounces and furbelows galore.

"Eggnog and song are our Christmas traditions here at the Sinclair House," Joyce continued, proffering songbooks. "We'd be pleased if you'd join in the singing."

"You wouldn't be pleased if you ever heard me sing," Corrie warned her, but she accepted the brightly covered booklet.

"She might be persuaded," Rachel said, "if you were to introduce her to that good-looking devil over there."

"Rachel!" Corrie tried to sound disapproving but had to fight back a laugh.

Some things never changed, she thought. Rachel had reveled in being outrageous in high school. More than a dozen years later, she was just as flamboyant, just as likely to say whatever popped into her mind, and just as unconcerned about what others might think.

"That's my son, Lucas," Joyce said.

"Is he married?" Rachel asked.

"Not at the moment."

A speculative gleam lit Rachel's eyes as she glanced, rather pointedly, at Corrie. Joyce caught the look and responded with a conspiratorial smile.

"Oh, no, you don't," Corrie said.

She'd have had more luck stopping a wrecking ball in midswing. Joyce bulldozed a path through the crowd, towing both Corrie and Rachel along in her wake, and neatly intercepted her son on his way to the window alcove that housed a grand piano.

"Lucas, dear," she trilled. "I want you to meet Rachel Diamond." Then, with what amounted to a flourish, she added, "And this is Corrie Ballantyne."

"Good evening, ladies."

His deep voice was compatible with the brooding hero of Corrie's imagination. She expected to find herself meeting dark, fathomless eyes to match, but instead they were hazel, a particularly appealing shade highlighted with flecks of green.

Joyce's painfully obvious attempt to play matchmaker was followed by her hasty retreat. "Time to dispense good cheer and songbooks to the other guests," she declared.

A moment of awkward silence followed her departure. Corrie said nothing, disconcerted by a whiff of bay rum. He'd really gotten into this turn-of-the-century thing.

Curious about him, her earlier interest deepening now that she was in his presence, she held herself stiffly so as not to betray any hint of what she was feeling. A mature woman approaching her thirtieth birthday should not have the urge to swoon when presented to a handsome stranger. Not in this day and age.

"Great costume," Rachel said, daring to run one fingertip over the velvet trim on Lucas Sinclair's lapels.

His professional innkeeper's expression never wavered. "You make quite a splash yourself, Ms. Diamond." His tone of voice was suave, and as rich and warm as a chocolate soufflé.

To Corrie, he said nothing. She felt a twinge of disappointment, forgetting for a moment that she did not want to attract his attention, but she wasn't surprised by the snub. Next to Rachel she often became invisible.

Bright colors had been Rachel's trademark even when she and Corrie were teenagers. Tonight Rachel's dinner dress was brilliant orange with a matching ribbon worked into her dark brown hair. Corrie was in dove-gray, a full-length cocktail dress chosen precisely because it conveyed a low-key anonymity. She could just imagine what the dashing Mr. Sinclair saw when he looked at her, if he noticed her at all—a woman of average weight, average height, average build, and average coloring with plain brown hair and ordinary blue eyes.

Perhaps it was time for a change, Corrie thought. After all, she was there on vacation. The problem with that plan was that her entire wardrobe had been chosen to fit her professional image. As a publicist, her job was to make sure her clients were in the spotlight. She stayed behind the scenes, going to great lengths to blend into the background rather than stand out. The only outrageous garment she owned was the hot-pink ski parka Rachel had just given her as an early Christmas present.

Then she sensed Lucas Sinclair's intense gaze settling on her. She had to fight an urge to fidget, and she felt a sudden empathy with animals in a zoo. When he spoke to her, his words were innocuous, a question about which of the costumes worn by the staff she liked best, but she avoided meeting his eyes when she answered.

"My favorite is the brown-and-cream number."

She gestured vaguely toward the fireplace, where she'd last seen the woman wearing that particularly elaborate dress.

When Lucas turned to look, Corrie did the same. There was no sign now of the wearer of the gown. Her gaze was drawn back to his patrician profile. For a moment he seemed puzzled, then he responded with a deep, rumbling chuckle.

"You must have spotted Adrienne," he said. "Would you like to be introduced to her?"

Still smiling, Lucas navigated a path through the milling crowd, until he and Corrie stood before the fireplace. There he indicated the enormous gilt-framed oil painting hanging over the mantel, a full-length portrait of a woman. Her gown was pale brown and trimmed with bows, its cream-colored panels embroidered in figures of red, yellow, and green.

"Ms. Ballantyne," he said, careful to keep the mixed emotions he was feeling out of his voice, "may I present Adrienne Sinclair."

He watched Corrie Ballantyne as she studied the portrait, trying to figure out what it was that drew him to her in such a disconcertingly powerful way. There was chemistry between them. No mistake about that. He'd known it from the moment he looked up and found this elegant woman staring at him from the opposite side of the Fireside Room. He'd quickly averted his gaze, but it had already been too late.

The intensity of that jolt of instant attraction had

both surprised and dismayed him, for unpleasant memories had rushed in behind it, rapidly transforming his reaction to profound annoyance, most of it directed at himself. His aversion to what he'd experienced wasn't Corrie's fault. She didn't know that there had been another time in his life when he'd felt this same kind of immediate, powerful sexual pull toward a complete stranger. She didn't know that in the first instance, he had made the disastrous mistake of marrying the object of his desire.

As he'd worked the holiday crowd, studiously avoiding Corrie, he'd been unable to resist sending swift, seemingly casual glances her way. What he'd seen had reassured him. She looked nothing like Dina, his ex-wife. Corrie had shiny medium-length hair, light brown in color. Though her conservative gown concealed her figure, he had the impression of a slender build and shapely legs. It remained to be seen if Corrie resembled Dina in other, less obvious ways.

No, it didn't, he told himself firmly. He was only standing this close to her now because his mother, up to her old matchmaking tricks, had pushed them together.

There was no reason he had to get to know Corrie Ballantyne better. In fact, if he had any sense, he'd avoid her completely during the rest of her stay at the Sinclair House.

Her friend, he noticed, had stopped to chat with another guest but was still managing to keep an eye on them. Another matchmaker. Resentment simmered just under the surface. Lucas did not like being manipulated, especially by women. That he'd already been attracted to Corrie before these two busybodies got into the act only made him more determined to resist her. He would treat Corrie the same way he would any other patron of the hotel.

Aware he'd been silent too long and that Corrie was slanting him a quizzical look, he launched into the patter he usually gave to people viewing this portrait. "Adrienne Sinclair was my great-great-grandmother, married to the first Lucas Sinclair. She and her husband expanded what until then had been only a small country inn. Within ten years, with the help of over three hundred employees, the place was a completely self-contained grand hotel with rooms for four hundred and fifty guests. Together Lucas and Adrienne made the Sinclair House a world-renowned resort. A hundred years ago you couldn't have walked through our lobby without spotting some famous person or other. Financiers, lumber barons, politicians, princes—they all came to the Sinclair House to be pampered. And to drink the healing waters of Sinclair Spring. The only thing that really compares nowadays is the luxury you find on a cruise ship."

"Amazing how she's re-created the gown in such detail," Corrie murmured. "Even the bustle and the accessories."

She was staring at the portrait with rapt interest. Frowning, Lucas looked at the painted gloves, the slippers with the ornate buckles, the fan. Then he studied Corrie's face again. He was obviously missing something. Her comment had been a complete non sequitur. "What do you mean by 're-create'?" he asked.

"Well, it says here"—she pointed to a small brass plate set into the bottom of the picture frame—"that Adrienne was born in 1847 and died in 1897. So obviously she's not the one wearing this dress tonight."

"No one is wearing this dress tonight."

"Someone is," Corrie insisted. "Or one very like it. I saw her standing right here not twenty minutes ago."

"I don't believe so, Ms. Ballantyne. A trick of the light, perhaps? You saw the portrait and thought Adrienne was a real woman?"

He could see in eyes the color of the first forget-me-nots of spring that she was annoyed by his comment. Her reaction intrigued him. Perhaps, he thought, she wasn't any more enthusiastic about being the subject of a matchmaking experiment than he was. And yet she was not indifferent to him. In the instant before she blinked and looked away, he caught the reflection of his own desire in her beautiful eyes.

She'd be there only a short while and then gone again, he reminded himself. He'd always made it a policy not to indulge in flings, and he'd long since vowed never to marry again.

Lucas Sinclair had no intention of letting history repeat itself.

"I know what I saw," Corrie said.

"There is no one here tonight portraying Adrienne," he told her, sure of his facts. "I would know. I arrange for all the costume rentals."

"Are you positive you've seen every single person at the party? There's quite a crowd."

Lucas's genial veneer slipped a little. He felt off balance, oddly uncertain in Corrie's presence. Most uncharacteristically, he spoke his first thought aloud. "Just how much of my mother's famous rum-laced eggnog did you drink before you saw this woman?"

As soon as the words were out, he knew the remark had been both rude and uncalled for. Even if it was the correct explanation, Corrie would be fully justified in taking offense. Instead, although her eyes narrowed, she remained calm, and what she said showed remarkable insight.

"I suppose you think if you irritate me, it will discourage me from being interested in you. There's no need. Let's not beat around the bush. We both caught that look your mother and my friend Rachel exchanged when we were introduced."

"They meant well. Still, I—"

Corrie waved off his attempt to apologize. "They may have romantic ideas, Mr. Sinclair, but I do not. I am not in the market for a husband or a love affair." She hesitated, as if uncertain she wanted to go on, then blurted out the rest of what was on her mind. "Just because you're reasonably good-looking and obviously wealthy, you needn't think that every plain little woman in the world will automatically fall at your feet!"

Plain little woman?

Startled to hear her speak of herself in those terms, Lucas forgot that he'd been looking for an excuse to put some distance between them. Suddenly he wanted to pursue this conversation.

A commotion at the entrance to the Fireside Room prevented him. Once he saw what was happening and recognized their unexpected and unwelcome guest, he had no choice but to abandon Corrie and resume his duties as manager of the hotel.

"Excuse me," he muttered, and left Corrie's side with more abruptness than was polite.

He was still peripherally aware of her, staring after him in confusion as he walked away. He was also cognizant of other guests at the party, and smiled pleasantly at one and all as he wove his way through the crowd toward the door. But the focus of his attention was an obsequious little man in a black suit, a man who was raising Joyce Sinclair's hand to his lying lips and kissing it in a mockery of that gallant gesture of respect.

With speed and efficiency, Lucas intervened, slipping an arm around his mother's shoulders and easing her away from the oily grip of Stanley Kelvin. "I'm surprised you had the nerve to show up here, Kelvin," he said.

What Lucas wanted to do was pick the rat up by the scruff of his neck and hurl him into the nearest snowbank, but the hotel didn't need any more bad publicity, and Kelvin was just the sort who'd jump at the chance to file a lawsuit. Lucas contented himself with a threatening glower.

"This is an open house," Kelvin said with a smirk.

"You invited the whole town of Waycross Springs. That means I'm welcome too."

"Everyone *is* welcome," Joyce said before Lucas could deny Kelvin entry. "Now, if you'll excuse me, Stanley, I must go check on Hugh. I'm afraid I've been neglecting him." With a speaking glance at her son, she hurried off. Hugh, Lucas's father, was confined to a wheelchair, but he had a clear view of all the goings-on. If he'd witnessed Kelvin slobbering a kiss on his wife's hand, he'd be upset. That had probably been Kelvin's intention.

"How is old Hugh?" the intruder asked.

Controlling the urge to throw a punch that would erase that supercilious smile, Lucas kept his voice level. "My father is recovering." No thanks to you, he added silently. "Why are you really here, Kelvin?"

The bitterness in the other man's voice took Lucas aback. "I can't afford to pass up free food, Sinclair." With that he pushed past his reluctant host and headed for the buffet table.

"Trouble in paradise?" Rachel asked as she joined Corrie at the hearth. "I thought you'd have tall, dark, and handsome eating out of your hand by now."

"I'd rather he use a plate."

"Oops. He didn't like being set up, huh?"

"You could say that. Neither did I."

"Darn." Rachel grumbled. "I'd have sworn I saw sparks between the two of you."

Corrie said nothing. She didn't want to encourage

her friend, yet she couldn't deny to herself that something had been simmering between them, a powerful attraction that defied reasonable explanation. She couldn't imagine why she should be drawn to Lucas Sinclair, not when he had that superior, know-it-all attitude. She hated that in a man.

A stir in the crowd signaled that Lucas was making his way to the Steinway situated in one of the room's many window alcoves. The singing was about to begin.

"Come on, Corrie," Rachel said. "If I have the chutzpah to sing Christmas carols on Christmas Eve, you can belt out a few lyrics too."

"Rachel, don't you remember? I sound like a dying frog when I sing."

"Oh." Rachel's stricken expression told Corrie that her old friend was indeed recalling some past occasion when she'd heard Corrie's attempts to sing. "Well, you can move your lips, can't you? Just mouth the words."

Rachel began to flip through the songbook, perusing the lyrics and keeping up a steady flow of irreverent wisecracks, until a red-vested waiter appeared at her elbow and offered refills of rum-laced eggnog. Corrie waved him away. She'd been drinking hers plain and after Lucas's nasty remark, she wasn't about to start imbibing the hard stuff.

The first familiar notes of "Deck the Halls" sounded from the alcove. Singing started hesitantly, but soon picked up both energy and volume as Lucas Sinclair's deep, rich baritone took the lead.

Corrie stuck to her resolve not to sing. She also made a concerted effort to dismiss Lucas Sinclair from her mind. As the singing continued, she thought she was succeeding.

The Fireside Room combined the ambiance of a bygone era with the atmosphere of a holiday party held in a private home. It had been decorated with all the traditional trappings of a typical New England Christmas—wreaths, boughs, pinecones, and the inevitable tree. The other guests were so friendly that Corrie soon felt as if many of them were old acquaintances. She was ensconced on one of the comfortable couches near the fireplace, exchanging gingerbread recipes with a schoolteacher from Topeka, when she once again caught sight of the woman wearing Adrienne Sinclair's gown.

The costumed figure stood alone, partly in shadow, at the opposite side of the large room. Corrie considered going over to the piano and tapping Lucas on the shoulder. He couldn't miss the woman if he looked up from his music. But she was comfortable where she was. Let Lucas think what he wanted, she decided. It didn't matter to her.

She watched the Adrienne-clone until the song ended, thinking that the woman's costume made the others look like cheap fancy dress. Even at this distance, Corrie could see that the gown was incredibly detailed, and that it appeared to be exactly like the one in the portrait.

A chorus of cheers and heartfelt applause heralded a change in pianists. Corrie joined in the applause and watched as Joyce replaced Lucas at the keyboard. After he began to circulate, still singing, Corrie glanced back at the spot where she'd last seen Adrienne's gown. She blinked in confusion, for in the minute that her attention had been elsewhere, the mysterious woman seemed to have vanished into thin air.

The Sinclair House's resident ghost sighed deeply, a sound no one but Corrie Ballantyne could even hope to hear. Adrienne knew she needed to conserve energy. She'd have to content herself with watching the rest of what went on in the Fireside Room from a dematerialized state. Remaining solid sapped too much of her strength.

Still, it had been enough. Corrie had seen her. Twice. For the first time in fifty years, someone had come to the Sinclair House who could not only sense Adrienne's presence but also perceive her as she had been, a corporeal being, as real as anyone else in the room.

Quiet elation filled her. She now had the opportunity to set things right. If she succeeded, she would finally be allowed to rejoin her husband, her Lucas, in the hereafter. They'd been separated for such a long time, over a hundred years.

Thinking of Lucas made Adrienne wonder if Corrie's sensitivity to the paranormal, already strong, would increase if she became intimate with a Sinclair male. Without any interference from Adrienne, Corrie had already caught the attention of Adrienne's great-great-grandson, the second Lucas Sinclair. About time the boy showed an interest in someone, Adrienne thought. And Corrie wasn't indifferent to him, either. She resolved then and there to do everything in her power to bring the two of them together. Kill two birds with one stone, as it were.

Adrienne was smiling as she settled in to watch the romance unfold.

TWO

"How's Pop this morning?" Lucas asked his mother as she arrived for work at the registration desk. In the hotel business, Christmas was just another working day. Lucas had been at the Sinclair House since six.

"Hugh is as well as can be expected," Joyce said, smiling wryly. "The evening tired him, of course, but I think it did him good to get out of the house for a while. It's important to include him, even if he did have to be in a wheelchair. I know he misses being here at the hotel every day. The Sinclair House has always played such a big part in his life."

Lucas hesitated, then asked, "Do you think he realizes the . . . difficulties he left us to deal with?" His father had suffered a stroke several months earlier, and his recovery had been slow. Hugh had almost entirely lost his ability to communicate.

Joyce shrugged, avoiding Lucas's eyes. She hung up her coat and hat, exchanged her boots for shoes, and went straight to the computer terminal. "It's hard to say for sure, my dear."

"Mom, we need to talk about this. Soon. This isn't the first time Pop has—"

"Could we discuss it later? Right now I have to enter these reservations into the computer."

Lucas skimmed the information coming up on the monitor as his mother typed. His eyebrows lifted higher and higher. " 'Cozies Unlimited'?" he read from the screen. "What kind of organization is that?"

Joyce's whole face lit up as she glanced at her son. "It's a conference for mystery fans. They're planning to hold a murder here."

"I beg your pardon?"

"They've reserved rooms for their annual mystery weekend in early May, and there are enough people coming to nearly fill the entire hotel. Isn't that wonderful?"

His expression darkening, Lucas put his hands on his mother's shoulders and turned her around to face him. "Early May? Mom, what were you thinking?"

"That over four hundred people will pay us to stay here and attend the conference."

"They'll freeze."

"Now, Lucas, most of the rooms have lovely fireplaces, and May is—"

"Not guaranteed to be warm. Besides, some of those fireplaces haven't been used for heating in years. Some of them are blocked off, by order of the fire inspector. We—"

"We have to find a source of income, Lucas. We

have to. How else are we going to pay for all the renovations Hugh had done?"

At the glimmer of tears in his mother's eyes, Lucas stopped berating her. Distractedly, he combed his fingers through his hair. "It's okay. We'll cope with it when the time comes. Maybe we'll luck out on the weather."

"I'm sorry, Lucas. I thought it would help. We do need business, especially conferences and conventions. You said that yourself."

"Yes, I did."

"Maybe they won't mind. They only sleep in the rooms, after all. The winterized section of the hotel will be all toasty and warm no matter what the weather's like outside."

"And if they do mind and complain, we'll have to refund their money or forget about ever attracting any other groups."

"Maybe the fact that we gave them such a good deal will make them tolerant." She indicated the screen, and Lucas felt his heart stop, then resume beating again.

Sometimes he wished they could go back to a simpler time, when no one tried to keep a summer resort open after Labor Day. At the turn of the century, the high season ran from July tenth to September tenth. You made your money then or you folded.

Folding was all too real a danger nowadays.

Joyce nibbled nervously on her lower lip as she watched him. "It seemed like a good idea at the time. Attract new business. Get out of debt."

"Mom," he said gently, "will you promise to let me handle this sort of thing from now on? You're a great manager for the restaurant and a terrific hostess, but now that Pop's out of commission, why don't I take charge of the bookings?"

"You've already got too many things on your plate," she pointed out. "What we really need is someone on staff to do nothing but scout new business."

"We can't afford that."

"We can't afford not to come up with some new ideas, good ones, and soon."

"At least next time you get a great idea, put me in the picture before you commit the hotel. Please?"

"Of course, my dear. In fact I'd intended to talk to you today about something. I want to explore the possibility of hiring a publicist."

"Where did that notion come from?"

"One of our guests does public relations work for a living. I saw her business card when she registered. It's that nice Corrie Ballantyne. You remember? That quiet, pretty woman. Why don't I invite her to have Christmas dinner with us tonight in the main dining room? I'm sure she wouldn't mind talking shop."

"And that's the only thing you have planned?" Lucas didn't bother to conceal his skepticism.

"Why, dear, whatever else could there be?" She blinked up at him in a feigned confusion that wouldn't have fooled a child.

"Give it up, Mom. Besides, I don't have time to have dinner with Ms. Ballantyne today. Neither do you." She served as hostess in the main dining room during midday and evening meals.

"Today is well planned," she answered. "No one needs supervision."

Lucas wasn't so sure of that, but he didn't argue with his mother. "Well, then, why don't you take some time off and spend it with Pop?"

"Because your father is going to be here again, when he wakes up. You and Corrie could join us for dinner and we could—"

"No, Mom."

"At least promise me that you'll take a little time for yourself today. You've been working entirely too hard. Leave the hotel and do something relaxing." When he started to protest, she added the one argument he couldn't counter. "You know what all work and no play did to your father."

Lucas considered her request. He could catch up on paperwork as easily at home as in his office at the hotel. He was about to say so when a sound made him look up.

Corrie Ballantyne was descending the grand staircase at the far end of the lobby. She looked as appealing in sunlight as she had in the glow of the fire. Too attractive by far. Getting out of the hotel for a while suddenly seemed like a wise idea.

The Sinclair House brochure boasted of extensive cross-country ski trails, the first of which traversed what in warmer seasons was a golf course. At ten o'clock on Christmas morning, having made dutiful, strained phone calls to her father and each of her brothers, Corrie set out across the fairway.

She was looking forward to her first opportunity in years to ski without a horde of nieces and nephews along. For once, she would not end up buried in the snow by Maurice, her brother's overly friendly Saint Bernard.

Crisp, cold air, the hint of a freshening breeze, and bright sunlight combined to cheer and invigorate her. Rachel's gift had been designed for cross-country wear, lightweight and ventilated to make the best use of the heat her exercise would generate. It had a hood concealed inside the collar, but that was more to protect against wind than cold. After the first mile Corrie removed a pair of fluffy black earmuffs from one deep pocket and slipped them on to guard against frostbite.

The opportunity to catch her breath was welcome too. She stayed put for a few minutes, surveying her surroundings. Off in the distance some tasteless developer had scarred the landscape with four large bright yellow clapboard condominiums. She turned her back on the horrors of modern housing and took a trail that led into the woods. The unspoiled beauty of forest and mountain was in front of her then.

She could no longer see the hotel, either, although she knew it was just off to her right. She suspected some sort of access road was nearby, but it too was masked by trees. Close to civilization, she still had the sensation that she was all alone in the wild, which was exactly the illusion she'd been seeking when she'd set out.

As she glided through acres of white birch and evergreen, she caught glimpses of other skiers from time to time, but they did not intrude on her solitude.

In another half hour she was ready to call it a day. It had been some ten months since she'd last been on skis, and although she was hardly running to flab, neither had she kept up any regular form of exercise. When an A-frame-style log cabin came into sight, she was very glad to see it.

According to the map of cross-country trails she had picked up back at the hotel, this was not one of the public buildings. There were several of those scattered about, including an emergency first-aid center. This particular structure, however, had been included on the map only to mark the point where the trail turned back toward the hotel.

Corrie had traveled in a circle. Another few minutes and she'd be able to put her feet up in front of a roaring fire and order a hot buttered rum. That thought brought a smile to her face. She'd never tried the drink and suspected it would taste greasy, but she had just enough energy left over from the skiing to feel daring. First, of course, she had to reach the Sinclair House.

Intending to massage her poor, overworked calf muscles before she continued her journey, Corrie bent down. She had no warning whatsoever before she felt a stunning blow to the side of her head. Pinwheels of pain and light danced in front of her eyes, spawning a kaleidoscope of colors. With a sick sense of being caught in a vivid, Technicolor nightmare, she felt herself fall.

She was vaguely aware of striking the ground with one outthrust arm before she came to rest facedown in the cold, powdery snow. Then the world around her dissolved to black.

"What the hell is she playing at?"

Lucas stared at the crumpled form for a full thirty seconds before he decided there was a good chance something really was wrong with her. He was perhaps a hundred yards away, close enough to see her fall without being certain what caused it.

He'd been watching the slender, bright pink figure, distracted from his work by some sixth sense as soon as she skied into the clearing that passed by his windows. There was no doubt in his mind as to her identity. There could hardly be two parkas in that particular gaudy color among the current guests at the hotel.

His computer screen glowed at him, the cursor blinking, then began to roll to indicate he'd stayed in one place too long. With a series of quick, impatient jabs at the keyboard, he saved the file he'd been working on and logged off. Keeping his gaze on the motionless blob of pink, he slid his stocking feet into low boots and laced them with deft fingers.

She'd been headed back to the hotel. It had been obvious to him in the few minutes he'd watched her that she was tired from a long morning on the trails. Her speed had been slow and then, inexplicably, she'd stopped.

For a long moment she'd stood there, looking around. Then she'd stared straight at his cabin. Brow furrowing, Lucas snagged a down jacket from one of the pegs near the door. She'd seemed to stare right at him. Then she'd turned away. Then she'd fallen to the ground like a wounded dove.

Even if she did know where he lived, why would she think he'd be home in the middle of the day? And how could she have known he'd be watching? The angle of the sun made it unlikely she could see him through the window.

His suspicion that his mother was continuing to play matchmaker didn't account for everything, though Lord knew she'd launched more complicated schemes in the past. Joyce always had good intentions, but he cringed when he remembered some of the things she'd tried.

On the other hand, if he was honest with himself, he'd have to laugh at the idea that she'd been able to convince Corrie Ballantyne to come after him on skis. What conceit! Corrie had told him plainly enough the night before that she wasn't interested.

She could have tripped and hit her head. So what if there was precious little to trip on out there? He couldn't discount the possibility. Heart attack? Not unheard of, though she seemed too young for it. At a guess she was in her late twenties or early thirties.

When he reached the door he hesitated, debating whether to phone for an ambulance before he went out. He'd feel like a fool if she'd just fainted, and a worse one if she really was putting on an act for his benefit. Disgusted with his waffling, Lucas slammed the door behind him with such force that aftershocks reverberated in the crisp mountain air.

By the time he had his jacket zipped he'd crossed the driveway and reached the utility shed. It took only seconds to slip on and buckle the snowshoes he kept there. If she needed medical attention, he could carry her back to the cabin, then drive her to the hospital. That would be faster than waiting for the local paramedics.

With smooth, practiced strides, he crossed the snow. The closer he got, the more concerned he grew. It wasn't even possible to tell if she was still breathing until he was right next to her. The gentle rise and fall of her torso reassured him, but his relief was short-lived. A slowly spreading stain had already turned a portion of her gaudy pink collar bright red with blood.

Disoriented, Corrie surfaced through a steady roaring inside her head, convinced her face was being licked by a large dog with a wet terry-cloth tongue.

She thought it must be a Saint Bernard. Logical, really, since the breed had once been used to rescue lost skiers. Then she remembered Maurice. Certain her entire family was about to descend on her en

masse, she kept her eyes firmly closed. Maybe if she
didn't look, they wouldn't be there.

The faint aroma of soap teased her nostrils, mixed
with a second scent she could not quite identify. For
some reason that elusive odor filled her with an irrational fear. Her eyelids fluttered upward at last, as she
sought the source.

The world was a bit fuzzy, but she could make out
a decidedly masculine hand holding a wet brown washcloth. It was descending toward her face. Eyes widen-
ing in panic, she attempted to jerk away, but one edge
of the damp material caught her on the side of the
head. The mild blow unleashed a jagged shard of pain.

Out of some primal instinct for survival, irrational
but overwhelming, Corrie ignored the fire streaking
across her forehead and fought for her freedom. She
flailed wildly at both the man and his washrag, but
only succeeded in increasing her own agony.

"Settle down or I'll sit on you."

Large hands caught her wrists as the man tried to
immobilize her. Confused and frightened, Corrie ignored his deep-voiced command and continued to
squirm until, as if to carry out his threat, he slid closer.
She could feel the solid pressure of his hip against her
ribs. She was flat on her back on a sofa, she realized,
and nearly helpless against this stranger's greater
strength.

Frantic, she tried again to writhe away from him,
but the attempt only made him tighten his grip. Their
locked hands ended up right on top of her breasts. It

made no difference that jacket, sweater, and camisole prevented his flesh from touching her skin. Terror of another kind blossomed.

"Let me go," she whimpered.

She squeezed her eyes shut again as she went perfectly still. Her head throbbed unmercifully. She didn't know where she was or who it was who held her so tightly.

"I won't hurt you, Corrie," her captor said.

The voice sounded irritated and exasperated, but neither dangerous nor threatening. It was rather a deep, soothing rumble . . . and tantalizingly familiar.

"I was trying to keep you from hurting yourself," it continued. "If you'll stay quiet, I'll let go of you."

She took a deep breath, opened her eyes, and looked up at Lucas Sinclair. Her vision had cleared, and his efforts to restrain her had brought his face close to her own. She recognized that line of cheek and jaw at once, and if she'd needed any further confirmation, there was the dimple.

"Let me go," she whispered.

Hazel eyes flecked with green narrowed. He released her hands but didn't move away. No longer soothing, his next words sounded clipped, as if he was barely able to control the urge to shout at her.

"I'd advise you not to try to move your head just yet."

Gingerly, she lifted one hand to touch the spot on her right temple where the throbbing was centered. With hesitant fingertips she probed a surface sticky with fresh blood.

Blood. That was the smell she had been trying to identify. An involuntary shudder vibrated through her.

The skin had been creased and torn, but she quickly ascertained that the wound was not particularly deep. The moisture on her face was only soapy water. Lucas Sinclair had washed most of the blood away.

Head wounds bled a lot. Corrie remembered reading that somewhere. Her parka was probably ruined, not to mention Lucas Sinclair's sofa.

"Where are my earmuffs?" she demanded in a petulant tone.

Even as she spoke, she realized it had not been the most sensible question to ask. Typical, though. When she'd been in the third grade and had her tonsils out, the first thing she'd wanted to know when she woke up was what day it was. She'd been afraid that, like Rip van Winkle, she'd slept for years rather than mere hours.

"Earmuffs?" Lucas sounded incredulous as he repeated the word. "You're worried about your earmuffs?"

"They were new." She was still poking at the wound on her head. "Black. Fluffy. I'm very fond of them."

"Stop that." He pulled her hand away from the gash. "You'll only start the wound bleeding again."

He guided her hand downward until her arm was stretched out along the length of her body. He had to inch away from her to make room for it.

"Your earmuffs are undoubtedly out there in the snow, along with your skis and poles. I was concerned about getting you inside, not with picking up your gear."

"What happened to me?" Belatedly, the proper question to ask in this situation had surfaced. At first it was met with silence. "Well?"

"Don't you remember?"

Puzzled by the harshness in his voice, she watched curiously as he rose and walked over to a huge picture window. There his dark silhouette stood out in stark relief against the sky, which was about all she could see from her position. The view was pretty spectacular, though, an ever-changing panorama of sapphire sky and drifting clouds. The shape it outlined wasn't bad, either.

It came to Corrie then that she was inside the cabin. The building marked "private" on the map was a snug little home where the hotel manager lived.

"I remember . . . something . . . striking me." Her voice faltered. The suggestion she'd been about to make, that she'd been hit by a misdirected snowball, seemed absurd even to her. Besides, she didn't think anyone had been close enough at the time . . . except Lucas Sinclair.

Her scattered wits slowly regrouped. If he'd been in the cabin, then he had to have seen her fall. He'd come out and picked her up and carried her back inside while she was unconscious. The fact that snow was still clinging to her clothing, unmelted, indicated that very little time had passed since then.

Cautiously, she sat up. Her head still throbbed, but after a moment the ache began to abate, and she told herself that in a day or so it would be forgotten. She wished she could feel as sure that she'd also be able to dismiss Lucas Sinclair from her thoughts.

He had left the window. Behind her she could hear the sound of water running in a sink. He was rinsing the washcloth, rinsing away her blood. She shuddered a second time, then made a concentrated effort to think about something else.

The sofa she was sitting on was long and wide and comfortable, covered with fabric that felt smooth and expensive to her restlessly moving fingers. She risked a glance at the throw pillow that had cushioned her head. It was stained with what was unmistakably blood.

Her gaze darted away, to a chair, to an end table with a brass-based lamp on top, to a coffee table. The cabin looked rustic from the outside, but the inside had been furnished with comfort in mind. She risked moving her head a little and saw that bookshelves lined one wall, surrounding a built-in, state-of-the-art computer workstation. Apparently Lucas Sinclair maintained an auxiliary office in his home.

Drawing in a strengthening breath, she attempted to stand. The headache remained marginally bearable, but a sharp spasm of pain in her leg took her by surprise. Her gasp was loud enough that Lucas heard. She caught only a glimpse of him over the back of the sofa, as well as the tiny kitchen area to which he'd retreated, before she fell back onto the soft cushions.

His face appeared in her line of vision, and she was both surprised and gratified to discover that the long, lean features were fixed in an expression of genuine concern. "Lie back down," he commanded in a markedly gentler voice.

She ignored him and continued to massage the cramp that had caused her to gasp. It was already easing.

"What's wrong with your leg?"

"Nothing." She was not about to confess that she'd gone out skiing without warming up first. This man did not need additional reasons, no matter how petty, to think less of her. Any clear-cut reason why she should *care* about his opinion continued to elude her, but the annoying fact of the matter was that she did.

"What's your name?" he demanded.

"Forget it already?"

His lips twitched at her sarcastic response but did not quite form themselves into a smile. "I'm asking if *you* know it, not if I do."

"Of course I know my own name." She snapped the words out, suddenly on the defensive. "Cordelia Marie Ballantyne."

"How many fingers am I holding up?"

"Two. Happy now?"

"Not entirely, but at least your vision is okay. That was one of the things the doctor I talked to said I should check."

"You called a doctor? When?"

"As soon as I dumped you on the sofa and realized you really were unconscious."

This time her gasp was one of outrage. The arrogant beast actually thought she'd been faking to get his attention!

"He'll check you out as soon as I get you to the hospital," Lucas continued.

"I don't need to go to a hospital. I'm fine now." In an attempt to prove it, she flexed her leg, then swiveled until she could plant both feet on the floor. The movement jarred her head, and she couldn't keep herself from wincing.

"Sure you are."

Disapproval had etched a frown into his face, but neither his attitude nor her irritation with him nor her physical discomfort could prevent her from noticing how good the dratted man looked in casual clothes. Snug, faded jeans and a crewneck sweater hugged the hard, muscular lines of his body.

His fingers made featherlight contact with the side of her head. She jumped, her nerve endings all aquiver. It was not a reaction to pain. In fact, her head was hurting less with each passing second.

"Someone who knows something about head wounds needs to examine that gash," he said.

"I'm sure it looks worse than it is." Corrie hated having people fuss over her. "If I decide I need a doctor, I can get one on my own."

"I can't take the risk that you may suffer some delayed reaction." For a moment she thought he was truly concerned about her health. Then he added, "Or that you'll decide to sue the hotel for negligence."

Infuriated, she batted his hand away. "I suppose next you'll say I knocked myself out as part of some scam."

The odious man actually seemed to be considering that possibility. Determined not to put up with his nonsense for another minute, she tried once again to get up. This time a wave of dizziness swamped her before she could reach her feet.

Instantly, Lucas's hands clamped down on her shoulders. His grip was all that kept her upright.

"I'm fine," she insisted.

"You're stubborn," he corrected her. Gently but firmly, he used that same hold to force her back against the sofa cushions. "Were you that way before you fell on your head?"

She blinked up at him in confusion. For the first time she really thought about what she could remember. It didn't seem possible she could have gotten this injury from a fall. She'd been standing still. Blacking out and somehow injuring herself in the process made no sense at all. Her recollection of the few seconds before she'd lost consciousness was pretty disjointed, but she honestly couldn't think of any good reason why she should have ended up out cold in the cold . . . unless something had struck her on the head first.

"Did you actually see me fall?"

His grip tightened on her shoulders for just a moment before he relaxed his fingers, but he left his hands where they were. The contact began to have an unsettling effect on Corrie's heart rate. That sudden, deep awareness of his warmth and strength made her nervous. It wasn't like her to respond in such a basic, physical way to a man.

"Did you see me fall?" she repeated. "What do you think happened?"

"Damned if I know." He continued to hold her, as if to prevent her from making any further attempts to get up too soon. His fingers gently clenched and un-clenched on her shoulders. His eyes were intent as he studied her flushed face. "I'll tell you one thing, though. It scared the hell out of me when you didn't get up again. The only thing I can figure is that there must have been a rock buried in the snow. You must have hit your head on that after you . . . fainted."

For the moment she let his skepticism pass without comment. "Did you find a rock?"

"I didn't look for one."

"Then I guess I'll have to do it." She glanced pointedly at one of his hands, then the other.

He slowly released her shoulders. His expression gave nothing away, but after a moment he sighed with resignation and stood. "I'll go, and I'll retrieve your precious earmuffs while I'm at it, but as soon as I've done that, we head for the hospital."

Corrie said nothing, but she didn't much care for the way he was ordering her about.

After Lucas had shrugged into a down jacket and slammed out the door, she got to her feet. The room swayed, then steadied. She took a moment to examine her surroundings more carefully. There was a sleeping loft on the second level. What she could see of a huge cathedral window beyond a king-size bed indicated that Lucas woke up every morning to a fantastic panorama. On a clear day like this one he could probably see all the way to Mount Washington in neighboring New Hampshire.

Dropping her gaze, she contemplated the view through the window in front of her. No other buildings were in sight, only the snow-covered cross-country course and the trees all around. The woods were quite thick just beyond the spot where she'd fallen. As she watched, Lucas collected her skis and poles, hunted up her earmuffs, and gave the surrounding terrain a cursory glance. The scowl he sent in her direction afterward was not reassuring. She limped back to the sofa and was sitting primly, her hands folded in her lap, when he returned.

Still scowling as he came through the door, Lucas announced that it was time to head for the hospital. He let Corrie get up by herself, but he did offer an arm as they maneuvered the flagstone walk that led from the cabin to a van that was parked a few yards away.

"So, did you find the rock that attacked me?" she asked as he settled her in the passenger seat.

"No. No rock. No branch. No sharp objects at all. I don't know what you struck your head on. Maybe one of your own ski poles. A freak accident."

That sounded pretty far-fetched, but she didn't say anything else until he'd loaded her ski equipment into the back of the van and had slid into place on the driver's side.

"I didn't come looking for you," she told him, "and I didn't faint, either. I've never fainted in my entire life."

"There's a first time for everything."

After that remark, they maintained a strained silence the rest of the way to the hospital.

THREE

Lucas sat alone in the stark emergency room waiting area, shifting restlessly on the hard plastic chair. "Rule one of successful innkeeping," he muttered darkly. "Do not get too involved with any one guest."

"Need to talk to you, Mr. Sinclair." Officer Gordon Tandy looked unhappy as he shrugged out of his uniform jacket and took the chair opposite Lucas.

"What's wrong, Tandy?" The way his day was going, Lucas figured Corrie Ballantyne had decided to press some sort of charges against him.

"I just talked to Ms. Ballantyne's doctor."

"Why?"

"He was puzzled by her injury."

"What are you getting at, Tandy?"

"The crease in her temple is actually a shallow groove. He thought she might have been grazed by a bullet."

"That's crazy!" Lucas was on his feet, hands fisted

at his sides. "I can't imagine anyone discharging a gun for any reason on Sinclair land."

"Not even Stanley Kelvin?"

The suggestion made Lucas hesitate. As Tandy well knew, Lucas suspected Kelvin was behind all the petty vandalism, the bad press, and the odd rumors that had plagued the Sinclair House for the last few months. Lucas couldn't prove Kelvin was responsible for any of it. If Kelvin was responsible, though, it made a macabre kind of sense that having failed to do serious damage with such things as nails strewn in the parking lot to puncture guests' tires and annoying middle-of-the-night phone calls to guests' rooms, the vendetta might now extend to violence.

Lucas had no more logical explanation for Corrie's mysterious injury. Was he paranoid? Maybe. Suspicious at the very least. But he had nothing concrete to offer Officer Tandy.

"I'd have heard a shot if there was one. I didn't."

"That's what the lady says too." Tandy glanced at the spiral notebook he'd taken out of his breast pocket. "No bang of a pistol. No crack of a rifle. And you didn't hear anything . . ." He scribbled another note to himself. "Okay. That's all I need for now."

"Wait a minute. That's it? Throw out some crazy speculation and then let it drop?"

"Doctors have to report any suspected gunshot wounds. Cops have to check out the reports. I'm going to make a few calls, take a look at the ground where she fell. I'll let you know if I find anything, but it doesn't seem likely. Probably just a freak accident."

"Yeah." He'd said the same thing himself, but the possibility they were both wrong worried him all the same.

When Corrie came out, accompanied by the doctor, she was very quiet. Whatever had caused her injury, the physician's primary concern now seemed to center on the fact that she'd been out cold for close to five minutes.

"I wanted to keep her overnight here at the hospital," he told Lucas. "She refused."

"Pure pigheadedness," he muttered. He already knew her well enough to realize that he couldn't change her mind. Unfortunately, his comment made conversation between them stilted during the drive back to the hotel.

"I'll be glad to sign papers absolving the Sinclair House of all liability," she finally offered. He heard the hint of sarcasm in her voice and winced.

"I'll send my mother up to keep an eye on you," he countered.

"I am perfectly capable of setting an alarm clock to wake me every few hours. Besides, Rachel will be back soon. I'll be just fine. My head has already stopped throbbing."

"Liar. Dammit, Corrie! Stop being so stubborn. It's no crime to accept help."

At once she looked contrite, but she didn't apologize. Instead, she touched his forearm. "You've done more for me than you needed to already," she said softly.

Surprised at the touch, he glanced away from the

road for a moment to stare at her. She seemed about to withdraw her hand when he moved, sliding his arm free and at the same time capturing her gloved fingers with his own.

"I can take care of myself," she said in a faint voice.

Reluctantly, he released his grip. Whether she liked it or not, he now felt responsible for her well-being.

"My God, Corrie! What did you do to yourself?"

Calmly setting aside the newspaper she had been reading while she waited for Rachel, Corrie managed to keep her tone casual. "Like it?" She touched the fresh white bandage decorating her brow. "I'm thinking of starting a new fashion trend."

Rachel didn't say a word. She just stood there, hands on hips, boots puddling on the lobby's plush carpet as she tapped one foot and waited for details.

"It's nothing," Corrie said. "You know what a klutz I am. I fell. Tripped myself up on my own ski poles and impaled myself on the tip of one of them."

That did seem the most likely explanation, although neither blood nor torn skin had remained to verify it by the time Corrie got around to examining her equipment. She reasoned that since the poles had been lying in the snow until Lucas reclaimed them, the evidence had simply been washed away.

"A klutz, you're not." Rachel's gaze never left her friend's face as she peeled off the top layers of clothing she'd worn for downhill skiing at a nearby slope. "Have you been to a doctor?"

"Have I had my head examined? Yes." Levity was not working. With a sigh of resignation she waved Rachel into a vacant chair, arranged kitty-corner to her own, and offered up a more detailed account of the mishap.

She did not, however, tell Rachel that even the doctor had been puzzled by her injury. Or that the police had talked to her. She didn't want her friend to worry.

Her edited version of events fell far short of answering all of Rachel's questions. Corrie could almost see the skepticism growing as her tale wound to a close.

"You got overtired and fell?" Rachel repeated.

"Yup. Grace personified, that's me."

"Hah! Let me tell you something, kiddo. You are the most graceful person I've ever known. I've always envied you that. You're one of those disgusting women who can cross a tile floor in high heels and not sound like an army on the march."

"Thanks. I think."

"You're sure there wasn't some obstacle on the trail? The hotel should put up warning signs if it isn't safe to—"

Corrie held up both hands to stop the impending tirade. "Honest, counselor, the accident was my own fault."

"My reasons for asking aren't entirely personal." Rachel lowered her voice in deference to the other guests who periodically drifted through the lobby. "You know this is a working vacation for me."

Rachel had suggested they spend the holiday at the Sinclair House so that she could check out its facilities for the travel agency she owned in Brooklyn. If everything passed inspection, she planned to send business their way.

"You can recommend the Sinclair House to your clients without a qualm."

"So," Rachel asked next, "how did you get back here after you fell? And who took you to the hospital?"

A sudden blossoming of color in Corrie's face gave her away.

"Aha!"

"Okay. Okay. I was rescued by Lucas Sinclair."

Grinning, Rachel extended stocking feet toward the glowing hearth. Her boots had joined the pile of outerwear between the chairs. "Can't leave you alone for a minute, can I? Are you going to see him again?"

"Short of checking out and going home, I can scarcely avoid it."

A session in the whirlpool when she'd first returned to the hotel had eased Corrie's sore muscles, but just the mention of Lucas Sinclair made her tense up all over again. Under Rachel's close scrutiny, that nervousness grew. When she realized she was plucking at her sleeve, she forced her betraying fingers to be still. Silently, she stared into the fire, hoping Rachel would let the matter drop.

She should have known better.

"You want to talk about it?"

"My accident? I told you. I'm fine. The doctor at the hospital slapped a bandage on my head and warned me to take it easy for the next few days. It's really nothing more than a bad scrape."

"Not the accident, kiddo." Rachel sent a knowing look in Corrie's direction. "I want to hear more about tall, dark, and handsome."

"There is no more."

"You can't deny your encounter with him was unique."

"You're going to keep wheedling until you have all the salacious details, aren't you?"

"Are there salacious details? Oh, goody. Come on, Corrie. Give."

In the hope that putting her feelings into words might help her sort them out, Corrie finally confessed. "I think I'm in big trouble, Rachel."

"Tell Mama all about it."

Despite the fact that they were in one of the hotel's most public areas, their high-backed wing chairs gave an illusion of privacy. The crackle of the wood fire soothed and consoled and muted the sound of their voices. Still, Corrie spoke softly.

"Nobody has ever affected me this way before, Rachel. When I was in his van on the way to the hospital, I caught myself wondering what it would be like to go to bed with him. I've barely met the man. I shouldn't be having thoughts like that."

"Why not? Men have thoughts like that all the time about women they've just met. The only question you should be asking yourself is whether you want to do more than think about it."

"I couldn't."

"Shouldn't. Couldn't. Wouldn't." Rachel's teasing tone made Corrie smile in spite of herself. "You should enjoy already."

"It's only lust. If I ignore it, it will go away." Rachel just lifted one eyebrow. "Besides, I'm not the type to have vacation flings."

"Come on, Corrie. This is me, y'know. Be honest with both of us. What do you really, deep down, want to do about this guy?"

"Nothing."

Shaking her head over what she plainly considered to be an evasive reply, Rachel collected her things. "I need a shower and a hot drink." She started to leave, then came back and leaned over the back of Corrie's chair. "Has it occurred to you, kiddo, that if this guy turns you on that much, you owe it to yourself to go for the gold?"

"I'm not interested in chasing reluctant men, and that gold is as likely to be dross."

"What if he's the one doing the pursuing?"

"That's not going to happen. I don't think he even likes me."

Sighing deeply, Rachel let her chin sink into the chartreuse bundle that was her ski jacket. "Don't be so sure you're reading him right."

No one Corrie had ever encountered had come close to stirring her libido the way Lucas Sinclair did. It only took a look from him, and her insides turned to jelly. All the more reason to be wary of getting close to him.

"Probably best he stays cold and distant," she told Rachel.

"Distant, she wants! Just promise me one thing—if he does start to show an interest, keep an open mind. He might even be Mr. Right, y'know. You could end up married to the guy."

"Aside from the fact that I'm not interested in marrying anyone, did you take a good look at him? No man who is that handsome and still single is looking for a wife."

"So forget marriage. If you're really attracted to him, then you should treat yourself. A nice, relaxing, torrid love affair could be exactly what you need."

"In this day and age? Really, Rachel! We don't know the first thing about Lucas Sinclair."

That thought was sobering on its own, and perhaps the thing that finally convinced Rachel to drop the subject. Lucas looked healthy enough, but who could afford to take chances?

Suddenly Corrie had had enough of staring at the fire, and of futile daydreams too. It was a good thing Lucas Sinclair wasn't trying to seduce her, she thought as she followed Rachel toward the stairs.

Lucas hesitated, his hand raised to knock on Corrie Ballantyne's door. He could have phoned her room. This face-to-face meeting was unnecessary. More than that, it was unwise, given the fact that he hadn't been able to stop thinking about her since he'd delivered her back to the hotel from the hospital.

Something about her had gotten under his skin. He wished he could figure out what it was. Maybe then he could dismiss her from his thoughts and eliminate his unwelcome fascination with a woman who was only passing through his life.

The door in front of him opened, and Corrie gasped, startled by his presence. The sudden confrontation caught him off guard as well, so that for a moment he just stood there, staring at her, bemused to discover she looked delicious even swathed from neck to midcalf in another of the colorless dresses she seemed to favor. She smelled good enough to eat too. Something with a hint of apple in it.

"Checking up on me, innkeeper?" Irritation laced her voice, once she'd recovered from her surprise.

Good thing he hadn't been hoping she'd be pleased to see him, he thought. Aloud, he said, "Officer Tandy called. Your accident was more than a simple fall."

At that announcement, Corrie all but dragged him into the room, shooting a quick, guilty look toward the door across the hall. "I don't want Rachel to hear this." She hastily closed the door behind him. "I didn't tell her there was a possibility I was shot at. I didn't want to worry her."

Out of habit, Lucas surveyed the room, assessing whether the maid had been in to clean and tidy and taking note that the fruit basket he'd ordered had been delivered. That, he realized, explained the scent of apples.

His glance settled on the bed. A little later in the evening, someone would be in to turn the covers back and leave a mint on the pillow, but right now the bedspread showed the imprint of Corrie's body, suggesting she'd taken a nap. He was suddenly intensely aware that he was staring at the place where Corrie Ballantyne would sleep that night.

"What did the police find out?" she asked, breaking in on his wayward thoughts.

"Good news." He deliberately turned his back on the bed, only to discover he could still see it in the mirror over the dresser. "You weren't shot. At least not by a bullet. It seems you were struck down by a rock, after all."

Surreptitiously, he tried to get a look at the bump on her head, but she'd hidden the bandage by styling her hair a little differently. She seemed to be acting normally, he decided. A little testy, a lot sexy.

"Are you going to explain, or do I have to phone the police station for details?"

"How are you feeling?"

"Fine!" She glared at him. "Not even a headache. But you, mister, will be giving me a royal pain somewhere else if you don't tell me what Officer Tandy discovered."

"A ten-year-old boy was aiming at a squirrel with a slingshot. You got in the line of fire. When you went down, the kid took off in a panic. Tandy says by the time he turned himself in about an hour ago, he was certain he'd be sent away to prison for life. He'd convinced himself you were dead."

"Since I'm not, what happens to the boy?"

"Unless you press charges, nothing beyond what his parents decide to do to him. Tandy says he's already punished himself pretty effectively. Kid's apparently got a helluva imagination. He told Tandy that he was afraid you'd come back from the dead to haunt him if he didn't confess."

He expected a laugh. At least a smile. Instead, Corrie looked vaguely troubled. He hoped she wasn't contemplating prosecution. Yes, she might have been more seriously injured, but the boy hadn't intended to harm her.

"I know the family," he said. "My guess is that he'll be grounded for a month or two."

Was she even listening to him? She had a peculiar expression on her face, as if she was trying to sort something out in her mind and having no luck at all.

"Corrie?" Without thinking, he reached for her.

The moment his hand came in contact with her arm, Lucas knew he'd made a big mistake. Desire thrummed through his veins, disrupting every normal, rational thought process. A moment later, Corrie was in his arms, her lips just a hairbreadth from his own.

"This is a really bad idea," he whispered.

"Yes," she agreed. But she didn't try to pull away. She even swayed toward him as his mouth descended.

She tasted of the apple she'd been eating before he arrived. Sweet and tart all at once. Lucas fought back a groan of pleasure and lifted his head. She stared back at him, dazed, as he gathered her closer still, intending to make their second kiss last much, much longer.

Rachel's voice and her insistent pounding on the door brought his good sense crashing back. "Hey, Corrie!" she called. "Are you ready already?"

Corrie stepped out of Lucas's embrace. Her fingers drifted up to touch her lips, an innocently erotic gesture that sent renewed desire shafting through him.

"A really bad idea," she murmured. She looked shell-shocked.

Lucas wanted to deny his own words, to insist they were moving in the right direction with that kiss. Instead he apologized. "Sorry, Corrie. I was out of line."

The emotion that flashed across her flushed face might have been embarrassment . . . or disappointment. He couldn't tell, and there was no time to ask. It was enough of a challenge to recover his composure before she threw open the door to admit her friend.

"Well, hello there, handsome." Rachel looked so delighted to have found them together that he felt himself wince before he could get a professional smile in place.

"Good evening, Rachel. I just came up to see if I could escort you two ladies down to dinner. I've got a special table reserved for you."

He was smooth, Corrie thought a short time later. She'd give him that. Her own heart was still beating a little too fast as an aftereffect of that kiss. Brief as it had been, it had left her wanting more, but as Lucas guided them through the crowded dining room, he looked as unruffled as ever. She didn't know whether to hope it was all an act or not.

No doubt wanting her and Lucas to seize the opportunity to take up where they'd left off when she'd interrupted them, Rachel veered off before they reached their table, pretending to be curious about something she'd spotted outside one of the windows. Corrie started to follow her friend, certain it would not be wise to be alone with Lucas again, not even in a crowded room.

"You needn't fuss," she told him. "Any table is fine."

"You can dismiss me in a minute," he said, his grip on her elbow tightening. "First tell me what you intend to do about the boy."

She was surprised he had to ask. "Nothing. He didn't mean to hurt me."

Lucas gave a nod of approval and released her. "Good. I'll tell Tandy."

Corrie hurried away from him to join Rachel at the bay window, but of course Lucas followed her.

It wasn't difficult to see what held Rachel's attention. Across one end of the floodlit yard a brightly painted Santa Claus in his sleigh, pulled by a full contingent of reindeer, moved with mechanical smoothness on a track.

"My grandfather made that," Lucas said as he came up behind them.

A somewhat stilted conversation about Christmas decorations followed, continuing until Lucas had seated them at a cozy table in a window alcove. Finally, he excused himself to tend to hotel business. Corrie watched him leave the dining room and told herself that her sigh was one of relief.

Rachel gave a snort of disgust. "You're missing a golden opportunity here, kiddo. Handsome. Obviously well-off if he owns this place." She gestured toward the Santa and sleigh. "And the whole family appears to be disgustingly talented. What did he say? His grandfather built that?"

"Mmmm." That must have been Adrienne's grandson, Corrie mused as she picked up the menu. She stared unseeing at the selections, suddenly reminded that she'd dreamed about Adrienne Sinclair the previous night, an Adrienne who'd been to a ball and was in the process of taking off that same dress she had on in her portrait.

In Corrie's dream, Adrienne had slipped a lacy nightgown over her head, then climbed into a four-poster to snuggle next to a dark-haired, hazel-eyed man. The bed had been exactly like the one in Corrie's room. The man had been a dead ringer for Lucas Sinclair.

Think about something else, she warned herself.

"That light golden brown stuff is called bengaline," she said. "It's a heavy-ribbed silk, which gives it a corded look. And the panels with the cream ground are of lampas, another sort of silk."

Rachel gave her an odd look. "What on earth are you talking about, Corrie?"

"Adrienne Sinclair's gown. The one in the portrait."

"Oh." Rachel still looked confused.

No wonder, Corrie thought. Rachel hadn't been there when Lucas "introduced" Corrie to his ancestor.

She tried to shake off the feeling that something very weird was happening to her, but she wasn't entirely successful. She knew she hadn't gotten her knowledge of turn-of-the-century fabrics out of any book. It was as if she'd been there, with Adrienne. As if she suddenly understood what a woman who'd been dead for a hundred years had thought and felt.

Impossible.

But Corrie's sense of disorientation continued as she and Rachel ordered their meal and were served. Then, when they were halfway through the main course, Corrie looked up and saw her again—the woman dressed as Adrienne Sinclair. She was seated at the next table with a man who looked enough like Lucas to be his older brother.

Corrie blinked.

This couldn't be right. Both people were dressed in the style of the last century, but this time Adrienne wore less formal attire. The table was different from those in the rest of the dining room too. Larger. Covered with a lace tablecloth instead of linen. And bright sunlight illuminated the couple. Corrie blinked again, harder, but they were still there. And everyone else around them seemed blurry.

Adrienne smiled at her husband.

Then they were all alone in the grand dining room.

It normally seated two hundred and twenty-five. Corrie felt a hint of Adrienne's pride as she surveyed her surroundings. Each heavy table was flanked by ten high-backed armchairs. The best tables had a view through the picture window at one end of the hundred-and-fifty-foot-long room.

"Tell me your new scheme," the man said.

No. Not just any man, Corrie thought. Lucas Sinclair. An older Lucas, beginning to go gray.

"I think we should have an artesian well put in," Adrienne answered. "The water tank can be concealed in the woods above the hotel. Out of sight. The same way he hide the laundry room in the barn." What guests could not see, they did not have to think about.

"The spring provides plenty of water for all the hotel's needs. Why do we need a well?"

"Needing one isn't the point. Having two separate sources of water will emphasize the uniqueness of that which comes from the spring. We can bottle it. Sell it. Increase our income."

"Why go to so much trouble to convince people that Sinclair Spring Water is special? Your pamphlets have already accomplished that. We can commence bottling it any time you like."

Adrienne gave him a severe look. "I am serious about this, Lucas."

"Put in a well when we have no need to? Why, the next thing you know, you'll be trying to convince me to keep the hotel open all year round."

Genuinely appalled by the thought, Adrienne

jerked her hand away and put both fists on her hips. "Never! What kind of fool do you take me for?"

Behind them, a door slammed against the wall as it was flung open. Horatio Mead stormed into the dining room.

Adrienne gaped at her brother. He had not set foot inside the Sinclair House for over twenty-five years.

The collar of Horatio's shirt was askew. His eyes were wild. When he spoke, the words came out in a bellow of rage. "What have you done with my daughter?"

Corrie Ballantyne recoiled from the violence of the man's emotions.

Before her eyes, the scene dissolved until only Adrienne remained. Her shimmering shape floated for a moment in midair, then flashed Corrie a triumphant grin . . . just before fading into nothingness.

Gulping audibly, Corrie continued to stare. How had she just been able to see and hear a scene from more than a hundred years in the past?

Very faintly, as if from far away, Corrie heard Rachel calling her name.

Then Lucas Sinclair, the current one, spoke sharply. "What is it?" he demanded. "What's wrong?"

Corrie was painfully aware that neither of them had seen anything out of the ordinary in the dining room. Just as neither of them had seen the woman wearing the dress from Adrienne's portrait the night before.

"No," she whispered. "Not possible."

But there was no other explanation.

"Corrie? Are you all right?" Lucas had taken the empty chair at their table to sit next to her, all sympathy and concern as he leaned close and placed gentle hands on her shoulders. He peered worriedly into her eyes.

She forced herself to look at him. This was not going to go over well, but he had to be told.

"Lucas," she said. "I do believe I just saw your great-great-grandmother's ghost."

FOUR

Lucas's first thought was that she'd taken a harder blow to the head than any of them had imagined.

"I saw Adrienne talking to a man," Corrie went on. She had an earnest look on her face as she tried to explain her outrageous statement. "It was probably your great-great-grandfather, since you look just like him. They were sitting at a table right over there. And then a second man, a very angry man, came charging in and interrupted them." She paused, looking puzzled. "For a moment there I thought I knew who he was, too, but it's gone now." She touched her fingers to her forehead near the bandage and briefly closed her eyes.

"The doctor wanted her to stay overnight at the hospital," Lucas told Rachel. At the same time he reached across the table and took Corrie's wineglass away from her.

"Hey!" she objected.

"Just a precaution. If you're hallucinating—"

"I'm not hallucinating. I know what I saw."

"A ghost?" Skepticism laced his voice.

"Yes. A ghost. And this wasn't the first time I've seen her. There were two other occasions, both last night at the party."

"When you were drinking spiked eggnog."

"When I was drinking *plain* eggnog."

She bristled like an affronted feline, convincing Lucas that she believed what she was saying. He, however, was not so credulous. A ghost? Not likely.

The way Lucas saw things, other explanations were easier to accept, even if they were equally unpalatable. The bump on the head could be causing delusions. Or Corrie Ballantyne had come to the Sinclair House with some preexisting problem. A tendency to drink too much. Or a mental illness.

He sure knew how to pick them! In spite of the wild claim she was making, he still felt the stir of attraction just sitting this close to her in the deliberately romantic lighting of the hotel dining room.

Yet another explanation occurred to Lucas. She got points for originality if this was a pickup line, but if it was, she'd miscalculated. He'd accepted that a freak accident right in front of his place had thrown them together, but it was too much to expect him to believe she just happened to see *his* ancestor's ghost.

What irony, he thought. If she'd kept on playing hard to get, he probably would have come around. He'd already been reconsidering, contemplating asking her out. Especially after that devastating kiss they'd shared.

"Look," she said, "I know this sounds impossible, but I'm quite sure of what I saw. If you don't want to hear more about it, then fine. Go away. No one's forcing you to stay and listen." She caught a waiter's attention and asked for coffee.

Lucas kept silent until they'd been served and Corrie had downed half a cup of the steaming brew. "If you are going to talk about what you think you saw," he said in a low voice, aware of the number of people, guests and staff, who might overhear their conversation, "then I'm staying. After all, that's my great-great-grandmother you claim to have seen."

"*Did* see." She glared at him.

He glared back. "*Thought* you saw."

Rachel broke the tension. "So what did this alleged ghost look like already?"

Making a point of ignoring him and speaking to her friend, Corrie answered. "The woman I saw last night looked exactly like the portrait in the Fireside Room. Right down to the gloves on her hands. Then, and again this evening, she seemed as solid as a real flesh-and-blood person." Corrie took another long swallow of coffee and looked thoughtful. "I always imagined ghosts would be more ethereal. Transparent. Kind of floaty in their movements. If there were ghosts, that is."

"Second thoughts?" Lucas asked. Her claims were absurd. What a pity if such an attractive, otherwise rational woman chose to believe in the supernatural.

"Let's say I'm open to any other interpretation of the facts," Corrie said to him in a bleak voice. "I just can't think of one."

"There has to be a logical explanation for what you saw," Rachel said. "Maybe someone was wearing that dress last night. I mean, I didn't see her, but perhaps I just didn't look quickly enough."

"She was hard to miss. The bustle alone stuck out at least a foot."

Lucas started to interrupt, to say that no one at the party had been dressed as Adrienne, but he thought better of it. Corrie hadn't believed him last night. She wasn't likely to now.

To his surprise, she turned to him. Her hand trembled as she set her empty cup down in its saucer. "Convince me I'm mistaken. Please. The idea I've been singled out to be haunted does not appeal to me."

"You did hit your head," he reminded her.

She sighed. "That won't account for last night."

He felt as if they were going around in circles.

"So what we have here is a woman with a fabulous dressmaker." Rachel had steepled her fingers in the best Sherlock Holmes fashion, but she ended up sounding more like Sigmund Freud. "Hallucinations last night? The aftereffects of concussion today?"

Corrie shivered in spite of the warmth of the room. "But she seemed so real." She reached for her coffee cup and, finding it empty, signaled for a refill. "In a way it's spookier to remember what I saw than it was to witness it."

Rachel glanced at Lucas, deep concern for Corrie in her dark eyes. He didn't know what to say, to her or to Corrie.

"You two *should* have seen her last night," Corrie said. "Why didn't you if she was there?" Her voice caught. "That brings us back to ghosts."

"You really do believe you saw something, don't you?"

"Of course I saw something, Lucas. I wouldn't make such an outrageous claim if I hadn't. Trust me, I'm not the sort of person who wants to get her name in some supermarket tabloid." She made a face at the thought.

Lucas realized he believed her.

"Let's try being logical then," he suggested. "Have you ever been tested for ESP?"

"No."

"Previous sightings?" Rachel asked. "Unexplained phenomena? Things that go bump in the night?"

"No, and I haven't been exorcised lately, either."

"Don't go getting all huffy on me, kiddo. You did ask for help."

"Sorry." The waiter refilled their cups. Corrie all but inhaled this one.

"She always did have an active imagination," Rachel said to Lucas. "I can still remember her brothers teasing her because she watched a silly old adventure film on television and spent the next week looking over her shoulder for the Cyclops."

"*The Seventh Voyage of Sinbad*," Corrie clarified. She shrugged, looking embarrassed. "Even now, knowing how special effects are created, that monster still gives me the willies."

"Too much imagination," Rachel declared.

"Perhaps that's all there is to it." Lucas made the comment without much hope it would prove true. Life was never that simple.

"Nice theory," she said, "but it doesn't explain why my vocabulary suddenly includes words like bengaline and lampas. Those are two nineteenth-century fabrics, Lucas, but I shouldn't know that."

"Interesting," Rachel mused. "I never thought about this before. Do you suppose ghosts get to pick the outfit they do their haunting in? I mean, was that her favorite dress? Or did she die wearing it?"

"This is not helping, Rachel."

Rachel seemed uncertain whether to take her friend seriously or not, and Lucas sympathized. He was certainly having trouble buying Corrie's wild tale. She seemed perfectly sane otherwise, but there was no way he could believe her.

The waiter noticed Corrie's cup was empty again and returned with the coffeepot. As his boss, Lucas was glad the young man, a college student working on his vacation, was doing his job, but the constant interruptions were jarring, an unwanted reminder that they were in a very public place.

"The last thing you need is more caffeine," he told Corrie.

"He's right," Rachel said. "Another sip or two and you could go from just a little crazy all the way to meshuggenah."

"Fine. Gang up on me!" She stood.

"Where are you going?"

"I want to take another look at the portrait." She sounded a trifle desperate. "Reality check, okay?"

"Whatever you say," Lucas said, "but I'm coming with you."

Without the crowd of partygoers, the Fireside Room seemed vast and very empty. The Christmas tree lights had been turned on, revealing a new accumulation of pine needles on the carpet beneath. A small fire had been lit in the hearth.

"Hello, Adrienne Sinclair," Corrie said to the painted likeness. She glanced at Lucas. "A handsome woman, as they used to say back then."

"Striking," Lucas agreed. "Clever too. We wouldn't be what we are today if she hadn't taken a hand in running the place. She was the perfect wife for a hotelkeeper. A terrific hostess. Full of good ideas as well. She was the one who came up with the idea to promote the hotel by publicizing the wondrous properties of the water from our springs. She claimed it could cure everything from kidney stones to dyspepsia. Back then there were no regulations to make her prove it."

A stray bit of conversation flitted through Corrie's mind. "She wrote a pamphlet."

Lucas nodded. "We sell copies in the gift shop."

Disjointed phrases came back to her. "Was there a laundry room hidden in a barn?"

"How could you possibly know that?" Lucas

sounded annoyed. "No, don't tell me. Grandma's ghost provided that tidbit, right?"

Ignoring his sarcasm, Corrie stared at the portrait, telling herself it was just a lifeless face immortalized in oils. She saw that Adrienne had a dimple. Lucas's dimple.

"I don't know what I expected to gain by studying this painting up close," she said after a moment. "I suppose I should feel relieved that nothing strange is happening, especially if it only happens to me."

No ghostly figure had materialized.

She felt no unearthly cold spot.

The aura, or whatever it was a person was supposed to sense in the presence of the supernatural, was conspicuously absent.

Keeling over into a snowbank had turned out to have a logical explanation. Why couldn't this sighting?

Corrie wanted to believe that Adrienne at large was just a figment of her imagination, but she couldn't quite convince herself. After all, she'd seen her. Heard her. The only explanation that accounted for her sudden familiarity with nineteenth-century clothing was that she had encountered a ghost.

Corrie had never wanted to develop any sort of psychic ability. The fact that she apparently already had alternately intrigued and terrified her, especially when it dawned on her that she might not have any choice about acquiring more new perceptions.

"What do you want from me, Adrienne Sinclair?" she whispered.

Of course she got no answer. That would have

been too easy. The room around her was silent save for an occasional crackle from the fire.

After a few more minutes of fruitless staring at the portrait, she realized Lucas had left her side and was over by the door speaking with Rachel. It was obvious they were talking about her odd behavior.

"Great," she muttered.

Lucas glanced her way, saw her watching him, and cut short his conversation. "Call the front desk if there's any problem," he told Rachel as he left.

"What sort of problem is he expecting?" Corrie asked her friend when Lucas was out of earshot.

"Oh, you know. Raving madness. Stalking the other guests in their showers dressed as someone's long-dead mother. The usual stuff."

"Funny, Rachel."

"He simply suggested that a good night's rest might be the best thing for you." She gave the portrait a once-over. "So that's Adrienne, huh?"

"That's her."

"She's got one of those Mona Lisa smiles."

"More like the Cheshire cat," Corrie said, remembering her last glimpse of the ghost in the dining room.

Satisfied she'd seen all there was to see, Rachel headed for the lobby. Corrie followed. She supposed she might as well go to bed. She no longer had any enthusiasm for socializing.

"You don't need to fuss over me," she told Rachel when they reached their rooms. "It's not this little bump on the head that's causing the trouble."

But when she unlocked her door, Rachel followed her inside. "Humor me. I'll knock on your door every few hours. If you answer, I'll go away again. Feel free to yell whatever you like, just let me know you're not in a coma or anything." When Corrie started to object, Rachel cut her off. "Lucas and I are both worried about you. Live with it."

"Lucas Sinclair thinks I'm certifiable," Corrie muttered.

Rachel started to say something, then apparently thought better of it. Her lips thinned with the effort to keep her opinion to herself.

Corrie made a face at her as she got a nightgown out of the huge armoire that served as a closet. "Go ahead. Ask me how any rational person can believe in ghosties and ghoulies and things that go bump in the night."

"But you keep seeing . . . something. With a bustle yet."

"Maybe I am cracking up." Corrie frowned, suddenly remembering another detail. "Actually, this last time there wasn't any bustle to speak of. Hey, looks like ghosts do get a change of wardrobe. The second dress was made of blue serge."

Rachel whistled. "I'm beginning to believe you really are in contact with the supernatural."

As Corrie went into the bathroom to change into her nightgown and clean her teeth, she thought about that. She still wanted a rational explanation, but since none had presented itself she was stuck with believing in a ghost.

The more she thought about what she'd seen, the more details she could recall. For one thing, in the dining room that night Adrienne had looked older than she was in her portrait. Her dress had been for everyday, with a gored front on the circular-shaped skirt. It was an "outing gown," an outfit Adrienne considered appropriate for yachting, boating, and tennis.

"There was a jacket with a shirtwaist," she said. "Large sleeves. And a wide capelike collar trimmed with bias folds of ombré surah."

"What?"

Corrie caught sight of her own sheepish expression in the bathroom mirror. "Darned if I know," she told Rachel as she returned to the bedroom. "It just popped into my head."

"Sleep," Rachel ordered. "Lucas could be right. You did get quite a knock on the head."

Corrie obediently crawled in under the covers. "Lucas thinks he has the answer to everything," she grumbled. "I hope I am seeing ghosts, just to prove him wrong."

"He likes you more than he wants to admit too."

With a last glare at her friend, Corrie clicked off the bedside lamp and closed her eyes. "Good night, Rachel."

Gentle laughter reached her, along with the sounds of the hall door opening and the overhead light being switched off. "Good night, Corrie."

The door closed, but Rachel's voice was still perfectly audible as she launched a parting shot. "I was slow following you and Lucas to the Fireside Room because I stopped to chat with his mother," she said. "We're having brunch at her house tomorrow."

Lucas was just finishing his business with the concierge when Corrie and Rachel passed her desk on their way out of the hotel.

"Good morning, ladies." His glance encompassed both women, taking note of the coats and gloves they carried, but the moment his gaze fixed on Corrie, he stopped noticing anything else. She had an edginess about her, making him wonder if she'd slept any better the night before than he had.

Rachel returned his greeting. "Morning, Lucas. Have you heard a weather report? It looked kind of overcast from my bedroom window."

Storm clouds were gathering in more than the sky outside, he thought as he continued to study Corrie. She looked as if she couldn't wait to get off the premises.

"Chance of something," he replied.

"That perfect weather yesterday spoiled us," Rachel said.

"If we get more snow today, that should guarantee good skiing for the remainder of your vacation." Small talk! he thought. Suddenly he hated having to play the genial innkeeper.

"There is that," Rachel agreed.

Corrie still said nothing.

"So where are you ladies off to this morning?"

Rachel beamed, momentarily reminding him of a

schoolteacher who was pleased by a student's particularly bright question. "To your mother's house," she answered. "Joyce said we couldn't miss the place—a charming old Victorian just down the street."

Before he could think of a reply, Rachel grabbed Corrie's arm and propelled her out of the hotel.

Lucas bit back a groan. They ought to post a sign: Matchmakers at work. No wonder Corrie looked so ill at ease.

He tried to dismiss her from his thoughts, but for the next half hour images of Corrie in his childhood home kept slipping into his mind. It unnerved him to think what stories his mother might be telling her. He could be reading too much into a simple invitation to visit, but he had the uncomfortable feeling that he was not. Before an hour had passed, he had found someone to cover the registration desk for him and was on his way out the door.

He told himself he'd been meaning to visit his father that day anyway.

After a delicious brunch, Joyce Sinclair led her guests into a room filled with books on local history and what appeared to be bound volumes of every issue of *Down East* and *Yankee* magazines for at least forty years. Urging them to sit on either side of her on a long sofa, Joyce indicated the stack of albums she'd placed on the coffee table. "I thought you might enjoy seeing these."

Corrie's first thought was that Joyce was matchmaking again. She expected to be treated to Lucas's baby pictures, but instead the scrapbooks were filled with clippings, photographs, and memorabilia tracing the history of the Sinclair House. Joyce moved rapidly back in time, providing an impromptu history lesson. Decades flew by, all made vivid by Joyce's anecdotes. The most compelling sight was a black-and-white photograph that showed one entire wing of the hotel in flames.

"Nineteen forty-seven," Joyce murmured, pausing a little longer on that page. "The year of the wildfires. A lot of Maine communities were damaged. Fires raged out of control in hot spots all over the state. They came after a three-month-long drought, and in a cone year too."

Corrie wanted to ask what a cone year was, but Joyce rushed on, adding only that her husband and his father had risked their lives to put the fire out before the rest of the building caught.

A few minutes later, Joyce slowed down again. She'd come to a picture of her own house. "Adrienne and Lucas's son Norman built this for his bride," she told Corrie and Rachel. "After about 1900 the whole family lived here during the winter when the hotel was closed."

Corrie felt her interest quicken at the mention of Adrienne. "And before that? Did the family live in the hotel?"

"Oh, yes. In fact, the room you have now was once part of the family suite. Adrienne and her Lucas stayed on the third floor in the central wing of the hotel year-round."

Turning back another page, Joyce came to Adrienne Sinclair's obituary. A great sadness crept into Corrie's heart as she read the yellowed clipping. "She was only fifty when she died. That seems so young."

"Not in those days. Not for women. The Sinclair men, on the other hand, have a history of being long-lived. They all tend to reach their nineties."

Reminded of her own family situation, Corrie said nothing, but she wasn't given time to dwell on the subject. Joyce turned to her, an earnest expression on her face.

"I wonder if you'd mind telling me something, my dear. I know you're a freelance publicist. What is it you do exactly?"

"I handle public relations campaigns for several retail merchandise businesses. I also work for a library district and a children's book writer."

Joyce looked impressed. "That must be fascinating."

"I have no experience with hotels," Corrie warned her, but the disclaimer didn't discourage Joyce from launching into an account of her quest for new business for the Sinclair House. Adrienne had come up with a great gimmick with the spring water. Joyce was hoping to find a modern equivalent.

"You could always conjure up a few ghosts," Rachel said.

"Bad idea." Corrie's voice was low, a warning intended to stop her friend from blurting out anything more.

"Ghosts?" Joyce echoed. Dead silence lasted a full sixty seconds, then she clapped her hands in delight. "What a wonderful idea! We can hold séances. Maybe Adrienne will appear. I've certainly got plenty of questions I'd like to ask her."

"Get Corrie to pass them along," Rachel said. "She's already seen her."

"You've made psychic contact with Adrienne?" Joyce sounded thrilled. "Did you see her too?" she asked Rachel.

"I should be so lucky."

"Oh, my! A ghost. A real ghost. How splendid."

"So go on already." Rachel poked Corrie in the ribs. "Tell her the whole story."

Reluctantly, Corrie recounted the details of her three sightings. When her story was finished, Joyce leapt to her feet and ran to the bookshelves. She pulled out an old photo album and quickly found the page she wanted. "Was this the man you saw?"

Corrie looked down at an older Lucas, handsome as the devil with a touch of gray at his temples. "The first Lucas? Adrienne's husband?"

"Yes. The resemblance to our Lucas is remarkable, isn't it? Now, what about him?" Joyce flipped back a dozen pages and held the album out again.

And there he was, the man who'd been yelling at Adrienne in the dining room. "Who is he?" Corrie whispered.

"Horatio Mead. Adrienne's brother." Joyce

frowned. "I wouldn't have thought he'd have crossed the threshold of the Sinclair House, not for any reason. There was a feud between the Meads and the Sinclairs, you see. Each family owned a hotel. Adrienne abandoned her family's place, the Phoenix Inn, to marry the owner of the Sinclair House. The Phoenix is still in business, more or less. It's a ramshackle old place on the other side of town."

"Do the Meads still own it?" Rachel asked.

"A descendant does. Stanley Kelvin." Joyce blushed. "You might have seen him at the Christmas Eve party. I'm afraid Lucas left you to try to kick him out, but he didn't do it, of course. Not from an open house. Poor Stanley. His mother insisted that he take over the hotel after the death of her father, Erastus Mead. Erastus was Horatio's grandson. Poor old Horatio must have been spinning in his grave when Stanley ran the place into the ground. Which brings me back to what you saw, Corrie. Why on earth would Horatio have come to the Sinclair House?"

A flash of memory provided the answer. "He was looking for his daughter."

"Really?" Joyce seemed intrigued by that notion.

Corrie suddenly felt self-conscious. "I wish I knew how I know that." What she'd seen and heard in the dining room was coming back to her in bits and pieces like a dream. She could not remember all of it, though.

"Oh, this is wonderful. Our hotel with its very own ghosts." But Joyce's awe and delight turned to dismay at a sound behind them. A man in a wheelchair, the man Lucas had stopped to talk to at the Christmas Eve party, had entered the room without any of them noticing.

"Hugh!" Joyce exclaimed, rushing to his side. He was Lucas's father, Corrie realized. And she saw, too, that Lucas was not the only one to inherit striking good looks from a previous generation. What in his younger days must have been thick dark hair was now snowy white. Hugh's facial features, even ravaged by age and illness, were still handsome. His eyes, the same hazel color as his son's, looked alert and intelligent . . . and deeply concerned.

When Joyce knelt beside his wheelchair, Hugh made a strangled sound, plainly trying to speak. All that came out was an alarming rattling noise deep in his throat.

"Oh, my! You aren't supposed to upset yourself." Sounding shaken, Joyce sprang to her feet once more and wheeled him from the room.

The devotion of wife to husband was obvious, and painfully reminiscent of the way Corrie's mother had tended to drop everything to cater to Donald Ballantyne's whims. Corrie knew this wasn't the same. Hugh was ill and needed attention. Still, Joyce's behavior made her uncomfortable.

"Maybe we should leave," she said to Rachel.

They were in the hallway when Lucas walked through the front door. Corrie froze as his startled gaze went first to his mother, just disappearing into another room with the wheelchair, then to her.

"What the hell is going on here?" he demanded.

"Your father's a little upset," Joyce told him, popping back out into the hall at the sound of her son's voice.

Corrie cleared her throat, prepared to explain, but Lucas brushed past her to follow Joyce into what was apparently Hugh's room.

"Yup. Definitely time to leave," Rachel said.

They retrieved their coats and already had the front door open when Lucas reappeared. His piercing glare impaled Corrie, making flight impossible.

"We'll talk later," he said. "At the hotel."

For a promise, it felt suspiciously like a threat.

FIVE

Overcast skies, merely threatening earlier, had by midafternoon produced freezing rain rather than snow. Lucas stopped beneath the portico outside the front entrance of the Sinclair House to brush moisture from his coat and glower at the precipitation. Sleet meant slippery roads and an atmosphere of doom and gloom. Bad for skiing. Bad for tourism. Bad for the Sinclair House.

Perfect weather for ghosts, though.

He entered the lobby to find Corrie Ballantyne occupying a chair near the registration desk. She was only pretending to read a novel. He watched her for a few minutes as she stared at one page, never turning to the next.

After all the trouble she was causing, how could he still want to look after her? Protective instincts warred with his natural wariness of women. The whole situation was so preposterous that his normal decisiveness had deserted him.

"Ms. Ballantyne," he said softly. "Would you come into my office, please?"

A guilty start was her first reaction. Then she complied with his request.

Lucas's inner sanctum was furnished much as it had been in his great-great-grandfather's time, with a massive oak rolltop desk, chairs covered in garnet-colored leather, and framed maps showing nineteenth-century street plans for the state's major cities. A computer terminal was discreetly hidden in the shadows behind a four-drawer wooden file cabinet.

"Is your father all right?" Corrie asked.

Lucas hung his coat on the coatrack and seated himself in the massive chair behind the desk, waving Corrie into a smaller version situated to one side. He picked up a pencil, tapped it on the blotter, then tossed it away. He didn't want to look at Corrie. He was already too aware of her. The atmosphere in the office had the same charge that preceded an electrical storm.

"Pop managed a few words after you left the house," he said. "That's the first time he's spoken since his stroke."

"Lucas, that's wonderful." Her voice hummed with sincerity.

"He said 'ghost' and then 'girl saw her.' "

Corrie sat up straighter, drawing his gaze to her in spite of his resolve. "Girl? What girl?"

"That's what I'd like to know. Mom and I are pretty sure he didn't mean you, but he couldn't man-

age to say any more. He nearly made himself ill trying."

He'd gotten so agitated that Lucas had insisted
they drop the subject. He'd feared a second stroke was
imminent and called Hugh's doctor. Fortunately, Doc
lived only two doors away. Semiretired, he was Hugh's
friend as well as his physician. He'd advised rest and
assured them all would be well if Hugh avoided getting overexcited.

"Just how much of my conversation with your
mother did he overhear?" Corrie asked.

"Only the last part, what Mom said about ghosts,
but she was filling him in on the rest when I returned
from seeing you out."

Lucas had tried to stop his mother. She had over-
ruled his objections and insisted on telling the tale,
which had riveted his father's attention.

"After she finished," Lucas went on, "Mom asked
Pop if he thought you were telling the truth. He nodded his head. Then he managed those few words.
That's more progress than we've seen in weeks, but I
can't say I'm pleased by the cause."

Corrie leaned forward. Her fingers came to rest on
his arm in a gesture of comfort. Surprised, he stared at
them as waves of heat surged up his arm and into his
chest.

When she started to pull away, to release her hold,
he couldn't stop himself from capturing her hand.
Seemingly of its own volition, his thumb brushed
across her palm. He felt her delicate shiver. His own
reaction was both immediate and powerful.

He stared at her, thunderstruck. Why her? Why now?

For Corrie, the erotic shock waves began as a tingling sensation in her hand, then shuddered through her entire system. The embarrassingly sensual reaction was even more powerful than what she'd felt the day before when he'd touched her at the cabin, or kissed her in her room. She had to fight an urge to close her eyes and moan aloud.

She knew the smart move would be to extricate herself from his grip, but her willpower just wasn't up to the task. Instead she cleared her throat and tried to pretend he wasn't affecting her at all. The effort seemed futile when she realized he must be feeling the pulse leap in her wrist.

Slowly, he released her, his hand curling into a fist on top of his blotter. Corrie struggled against the temptation to reach out again, to seize his hand and restore that tantalizing contact.

Bad idea! Get back on track, she warned herself.

"As I was sitting in the lobby just now," she said in a voice that sounded a trifle breathless, "I was trying to think of an explanation for what I've experienced. Something other than the supernatural one."

"Any luck?" The huskiness in his own voice betrayed him. He was as affected by the chemistry between them as she was.

"Not unless someone's trying to trick me," she said.

"How?" He put more distance between them by rolling his chair to the far end of the huge desk. Absently, he aligned the day-by-day calendar with the edge of the blotter. Anything, she surmised, to avoid meeting her eyes.

The theory she'd devised while waiting for him was a last-ditch, rather desperate attempt to explain Adrienne away. She didn't hold out much hope it would wash, but she voiced it anyhow.

"Could a ghost be faked by using a hidden projector or something? I don't know a thing about high-tech special effects, but I've heard people talk about lasers and holograms. Sometimes it seems to me that just about anything is possible."

"Other people would have seen something if that were the case."

He was right. She should have realized that herself. "I guess it was silly to think anyone would go to that much trouble just to set up a hoax." She managed a weak, self-deprecating smile.

"One person might," Lucas muttered. "I'd love to be able to pin this on Stanley Kelvin, but I can't see him having the know-how to rig special effects. He doesn't have the cash to hire someone who would be able to do it, either."

Stanley Kelvin, Corrie thought. The man who'd kissed Joyce's hand.

At the image, she again felt the tingling sensation of Lucas's thumb on her own palm. A ghostly caress. How appropriate!

In spite of jangled nerves, she managed to speak calmly. "Will you tell me about him, Lucas? I saw the way you two looked at each other at the party. I could feel the animosity between you from all the way across the room."

"There's not much to tell. Some years ago, my father gave Kelvin a job here. Pop felt sorry for him and, I suppose, he might have been hoping to mend some fences."

"Your mother told us about the feud."

"Pop should have known better." With a sound of disgust, Lucas at last looked at her. His eyes were hard and lacked their usual sparkle. "Kelvin repaid his kindness by embezzling a small fortune from the Sinclair House. By the time Pop discovered what Kelvin was up to and fired him, we were nearly ruined."

Genuinely shocked, Corrie sagged back in her chair. "How awful." Almost as awful was the way her attention kept wandering. She'd come in there to sort out the facts about a ghost, but she was having a hard time keeping her eyes off Lucas's broad shoulders.

"He was prosecuted and did some time, but the money was never recovered."

If Lucas had seemed tense earlier, now he was drawn tight as a bowstring, but it was anger at Kelvin, not a reaction to her. Corrie told herself she should be relieved, that she didn't want his attention fixed on her that way.

"He came right back to Waycross Springs when he got out of jail. He was on probation for a while, but he's off it now. He's free to do whatever he likes, go wherever he wants. Until he's caught committing another crime."

It took Corrie a moment to sort that out. "You think he's up to no good?"

"I know he is, but I have no proof." As he told her of several instances of petty vandalism and crank phone calls, Lucas toyed with another pencil, then set it carefully aside, as if he feared he'd end up snapping it in two. "Kelvin would love to see us go under," he continued, "but he's not your ghost. He specializes in plain old-fashioned villainy."

"So that brings us back to a haunted hotel," Corrie said. "Your mother thinks the ghost has great potential as a publicity stunt."

Lucas looked as if he'd just bitten down hard on a particularly sour slice of lemon. "Oh, great," he muttered.

"She could be right."

"We don't need the off-the-wall clientele that kind of gimmick would attract." His eyes narrowed. "Why did Mom invite you and Rachel to the house?"

"Can't you guess? She was matchmaking again." It seemed horribly obvious to her now. "What better way to throw us together than to solicit my professional advice and then suggest, since I know nothing about the hotel business, that you show me the ropes?"

Lucas's expression was shuttered. "There's an easy way to extricate yourself from any plans my mother has for you."

"And that is?"

"Leave. I'll call around and find you accommodations elsewhere." He actually reached for the phone and started to punch in a number. "There's a nice old inn in Bethel, or you could cross the border into New Hampshire and stay at the—"

"I'm not going anywhere." Corrie didn't like having plans made for her in any circumstances, but Lucas's offhand suggestion made her stomach knot.

It was because she couldn't abandon Adrienne, she told herself. Nothing to do with the infuriating man behind the desk.

"If you leave you'll also be free of these sightings." Lucas still held the phone in one hand but he'd stopped dialing.

"*You* won't, however," she said. "Adrienne isn't a problem you're going to get rid of so easily. Sending me packing sure won't do it. If Adrienne is real," she explained, "then there has to be some reason she's haunting the hotel. I mean, everything I've ever heard about ghosts indicates that they walk because something horrible happened to them while they were alive. She must want to communicate with the living, and for some reason she's singled me out as her messenger."

Peculiar as it seemed to Corrie, the Sinclair House's ghost had chosen her. Adrienne needed her help.

Emotions flicked rapidly across Lucas's face. He looked as if he wanted to argue with her conclusion. She was sure he didn't believe she'd seen anything. But he couldn't be a hundred percent sure she was imagining things, either. Not after Hugh's odd behavior.

Corrie pressed her advantage. "Apparently I'm not the first to see Adrienne. You can't assume I'll be the last, either. If this matter can be settled now, with me, you'd be foolish to send me away."

He slammed his fist down on the desk, making the paper-clip holder jump. "Damn! I wish Pop could have told us what he meant. Who the hell was this girl? When did she claim to see Adrienne? What happened to her?"

"Let's try to find out," Corrie said. "There must be records other than those in Joyce's scrapbooks and photo albums. Newspapers. Local histories. The hotel registers. Somewhere there's an identity for this mysterious girl. And maybe a clue as to what Adrienne wants as well."

Corrie no longer had any doubt that she'd had a brush with the supernatural. She might have imagined Adrienne after seeing her portrait. She might even have guessed correctly that Lucas's great-great-grandfather would be his look-alike as well as his namesake. But she realized now, remembering Joyce's photo album, that there was no way she could have seen Horatio Mead's face before he appeared to her in the dining room.

"We know Adrienne wasn't murdered." Lucas sounded calmer and seemed to be taking her proposal seriously. "If I remember right, she died of influenza. They had terrible epidemics in those days, and no antibiotics."

Corrie nodded. She felt herself warming toward him again and decided she must be six kinds of fool. He was all wrong for her. But when she opened her mouth, it was to issue an invitation. "I need to know why she's haunting me. Will you help me discover the reason?"

Something that looked like speculation danced in the depths of Lucas's eyes, but it vanished before Corrie could analyze it. After contemplating her for a moment longer, he appeared to come to a decision.

"All right. Let me make some phone calls. I'll find out what resources are available. We may be able to start running down leads as early as tomorrow."

His words sounded like a dismissal, but they felt like an invitation. The man was wreaking havoc on her emotions. Her own confusion about just what it was she wanted from him made her decide this might be a good time for a strategic retreat.

As she stood, intending to leave, a slight movement near the file cabinet caught her eye. She froze, doing a classic double take. Adrienne stood there, her eyes fixed on Lucas.

"Lucas?" Corrie whispered.

"What now, Corrie?" Lucas's question was tinged with impatience.

Mutely, she pointed toward the oak file cabinet, but even as he glanced that way, Adrienne began to fade. A second later, she'd vanished into thin air.

"Damn," Corrie muttered. "You didn't see a thing, did you?"

"What am I supposed to have seen?"

"Adrienne. She was here, but now she's gone again."

"Did she try to . . . communicate with you?" He sounded as if he were strangling on the question.

"No. She just gave me that smug smile of hers. She's apparently pleased to have found us here together."

"Great. Like we need another matchmaker!"

Their eyes met. Renewed heat seared through Corrie, and she recognized an answering conflagration in Lucas's gaze before she forced herself to look away.

"Eventually they'll catch on to the fact that we aren't interested in each other." She all but choked on the lie and could feel guilty color creep up her throat and into her face as she walked toward the door. Her hand was on the knob when Lucas's low-voiced command stopped her.

"Wait."

"Why? There's nothing left to say."

"Yes, there is."

Corrie didn't think he'd moved, but she felt as if he'd come closer, as if he were surrounding her. She didn't dare turn around or release her grip on the doorknob.

"There's something you should know," he said. "I owe you that much. And an apology."

"For what?"

"For looking for excuses to dislike and distrust you. The truth, Corrie, is that from the minute I saw you at the party I felt . . . drawn to you."

Unable to stop herself, Corrie glanced over her shoulder at him. He was right where she'd left him, behind his desk.

"Our eyes met across a crowded room," he went

on, "and I felt an instant attraction. That's just about as corny as you can get, and as irritating."

Part of her wanted to believe what he was saying, the attraction part, not the irritation, but the rational side of her brain resisted. "Why irritating?" she asked.

"Let's just say you remind me of someone." He was toying with another pencil.

"Who?"

"It doesn't matter."

"It does to me." She was a hairbreadth away from confessing that she'd felt the same pull . . . and the same resistance.

"Fine. Her name is Dina. I used to be married to her." The pencil snapped in two.

If the atmosphere between them had been awkward and strained before, discomfort now took on a new dimension. Corrie's first thought was that he was still in love with his ex-wife. Her second was that he hated her guts.

"You are entirely too easy to read." He sounded disgruntled. "Let's set the record straight. My marriage was a mistake, and I make it a practice not to repeat my mistakes."

"So you gave up on women?"

"No. I gave up on marriage."

Corrie released her death grip on the doorknob and turned to face him fully. "I've told you before that I'm not looking for a husband. I meant that. You're perfectly safe from me."

His sudden grin rocked her. "Does that mean you want—?"

"All I want is to find out why I see Adrienne when no one else does."

A decided twinkle came into Lucas's eyes. For a moment Corrie thought he was going to come out from behind the desk and try to kiss her again. Instead, to her secret disappointment, he stayed put.

"That's that, then," he said. "I'm glad we understand each other."

"Right." This time she managed to leave the office before either of them said anything more.

He understood her? She really doubted it. And she certainly didn't have a clue as to what was going on in his mind. He blew hot and cold. One moment he said he was attracted to her. The next he implied he'd sworn off impulsive relationships for good. Then he twinkled at her! Was that supposed to mean he'd consider a vacation fling as long as she didn't expect him to marry her?

Muttering under her breath about charming, know-it-all men and throwing in a few choice words about meddling matchmakers for good measure, Corrie went to retrieve her unread novel from the chair in the lobby.

Of course he was charming. It was his *job* to be charming. She'd do well to remember that!

Inside his office, Lucas sat staring at the door for a long time after Corrie left. What was it about the woman that fascinated him so? And what on earth had possessed him to mention Dina?

Why he continued to be physically attracted to Corrie was a mystery to him. She certainly wasn't the most beautiful woman he'd ever seen. And she wasn't the easiest to get along with, not by a long shot. Prickly about summed it up.

And yet he felt this constant urge to touch her. He hadn't wanted to let go of her hand earlier, even though hanging on to it would have been faintly ridiculous.

Expressing his anger at Kelvin had seemed preferable to hauling Corrie into his arms and kissing her senseless. He'd probably sounded like a damned fool, ranting on like that. No better than Kelvin himself.

Corrie Ballantyne was turning him into an emotional basket case. This had to stop.

It would stop when they settled this ghost business, he decided, reaching for a sheet of paper. He intended to make notes on what he knew to date. There had to be a logical explanation. The most likely one, unfortunately, was that the woman he was so powerfully drawn to was seeing things that weren't there.

That fact alone ought to stop him from thinking of ways to get her into his bed. He didn't have time for this nonsense. He had work to do. A hotel to run.

Ghosts! Preposterous! He crumpled the still-blank page and tossed it into the wastepaper basket.

He could admit he'd had moments when he'd felt very close to his ancestors here in this office, relishing the long tradition behind him at the Sinclair House. Dina had once accused him of ancestor worship. But to actually see one of them? Communicate with her?

To all intents and purposes relive a bit of another person's life? That was the stuff of fantasy.

Not real. Impossible.

Was it also fantasy, he wondered, to think he and Corrie were likely to become lovers during what remained of her vacation? It seemed more likely that, at most, they were going to work together on a . . . research project.

Agitated, Lucas ran his fingers through his hair and turned to look at the corner by the file cabinet. How did one prove or disprove the existence of ghosts? It seemed to him that you believed or you didn't.

And he didn't.

Definitely didn't.

"Okay, Grandma," he challenged. "Here's your chance to convince the skeptic. If you exist, show yourself now."

When Lucas realized he was half expecting something to materialize out of thin air, he cursed fluently and stalked out of the office.

Early the following morning, Corrie awoke to find herself sitting bolt upright in bed.

"Jonathan Mead is a bastard," she said aloud.

As soon as she opened her eyes, her dream began to fade. By the time she was fully awake, it was gone entirely.

Except for that one thought. "Jonathan Mead is a bastard?" she repeated. "Who the heck is Jonathan

Mead?" And where had that thought come from in the first place?

Corrie assumed Jonathan was one of Adrienne's relations. The Mead family had owned the other hotel, but she could only remember Joyce mentioning Horatio, Adrienne's brother, and his grandson Erastus, who in turn was Stanley Kelvin's grandfather. No Jonathan.

Whoever he was, he'd apparently done some particularly mean and rotten thing, hence Adrienne's unflattering opinion that he was a bastard, a black-hearted scoundrel, the scum of the earth, a blot on humanity.

It had definitely been Adrienne's voice in Corrie's head. The more she thought about that, as she got up and dressed, the more certain she became that she had just received a direct message from the beyond.

How melodramatic that sounded, but it was true. What was in Adrienne's mind had somehow beamed down and touched her own.

The very idea made Corrie shiver. This supernatural link with a woman who'd been dead for a hundred years was getting way too weird. For just a moment she considered changing her mind. She could still take Lucas up on his offer to pay her way at another, similarly luxurious hotel.

The impulse to run didn't last. She knew she couldn't go. She was kept there by her sense of obligation to Adrienne, by her desire to understand why she had been singled out to have an occult experience at the Sinclair House . . . and by the need to sort out her decidedly mixed feelings toward Lucas Sinclair.

SIX

A snowmobile might have been more appropriate to use to check conditions on the cross-country ski trails after all the sleet they'd had the night before. Or snowshoes. Or skis. Instead Lucas chose the means of winter transportation Sinclairs had preferred for generations.

This particular horse-drawn sleigh, a Portland cutter, had been manufactured about eighty years earlier and refurbished just before the Second World War. It had been carefully cared for since then, even after the family stopped keeping its own horses. They stored the sleigh in a neighbor's barn, and when Lucas got the urge to take it out, Joshua brought it over and supplied the horse too. He was enjoying a visit with Hugh while Lucas went for a drive.

The previous day's bad weather had given way to sunshine and a gentle breeze. Lucas had been out for well over an hour and was heading back to the hotel when he caught sight of Corrie returning from town with her friend Rachel. There was no mistaking the two women, one in glaring chartreuse, the other in hot pink. The hotel laundry had apparently been able to get the bloodstains out of Corrie's parka. He had to smile when he saw she was also wearing those earmuffs she prized so highly. Her light brown hair puffed out at both front and back, looking soft and touchable.

He told himself he ought to keep going. He had work waiting for him, responsibilities. Instead he changed direction. Corrie and Rachel had just reached the stretch of sidewalk that bordered hotel land when he pulled up beside them.

The jingle of bells on the horse's harness caught Corrie's attention first. Then she stopped short, almost dropping her packages as she recognized him. She was carrying one of the heavy-duty shopping bags the local boutique gave out, with smaller bags bearing logos from other shops piled inside.

"Can I offer you a lift?" he asked, noticing that Corrie's cheeks were nearly the same color as her parka, flushed by exercise, and the crisp, cool air . . . and maybe by the fact that she hadn't been expecting to run into him.

"Doesn't look like there's room for three," Rachel said, but she had a conspiratorial smile on her face.

She was right. The cutter had only one double seat, upholstered in red mohair, behind the goose-necked dashboard.

Corrie said nothing, but she reached out tentative fingers to stroke the mare's satiny nose.

"Her name's Lavinia," Lucas told her. Nearly white, she looked striking hitched to the gleaming black-and-gold sleigh. She was also an agreeable creature who liked people. "Here, Corrie. Give her this."

From a pocket of his down jacket, he produced the apple he'd meant to feed Lavinia as a treat after the ride. He realized his mistake at once. The memory of an apple-flavored kiss was almost as vivid as the real thing. He cleared his throat and soldiered on.

"Hold your hand flat so she can lip it off without nipping your fingers."

He doubted she had missed the sudden huskiness in his voice, and she gave him an odd look as she accepted the piece of fruit and followed his instructions. "Did you make those phone calls?" she asked when the apple had disappeared.

"Some of them. It *is* Saturday." To his relief, he sounded normal again.

He felt anything but.

After a restless night, filled with thoughts of Corrie, he'd decided to humor her, telling himself it was only good business to pretend the guest was always right, even if he didn't believe this ghost nonsense for a minute. The truth was that their joint quest would oblige him to spend time with this woman to whom he was so powerfully attracted. Not an altogether bad thing.

"Come for a short ride," he suggested. "I can bring you up to date on my progress."

"It does look like fun." She hesitated, but he could tell she was tempted.

"Go, already," Rachel urged. "Pretend you're in a remake of *Doctor Zhivago*." She gave Lucas a wink and Corrie a gentle shove, relieving her of her shopping bag in the process.

Lucas held out one hand to help her up onto the high seat. "I haven't asked a woman to go for a sleigh ride with me since I was a teenager," he confessed.

Their eyes met over gloved fingers. He saw the flash of panic in hers but had hauled her up next to him before she could change her mind. He wondered if he imagined the look of relief when he released his grip on her to take the reins in both hands. He didn't think so. He knew already that she was not indifferent to him.

With a shake of the harness bells, they were off. Their progress was heralded by constant jingling and the soft *whoosh* of hickory-wood runners over snow.

"I've never seen *Doctor Zhivago*," Corrie said. "I assume sleigh rides are supposed to be romantic."

"That's the idea. They can also be entertaining. One of Mom's recent ideas was to offer sleigh rides to the guests."

"Is that practical? These days most people don't know how to handle a horse, and if you supply the driver there's only room for one passenger."

"It could work if we used a bigger sleigh. The neighbor who owns Lavinia here also keeps several other horses and he has a large sleigh that's something like a hay wagon. We could use that. Care to share your professional opinion? Would we have any takers for a hayride-sleigh ride?"

"I'm sure you would, but you'd do well to check with your insurance company before you start advertising it."

He couldn't help but laugh. "I hadn't figured you for a cynic."

"Well, you don't know me very well, do you?"

Something he'd like to change, he thought.

They coasted at a decorous pace across the snow-covered golf course and onto part of the same cross-country trail Corrie had used on Christmas Day. Everything had a crystalline pureness after the storm, for at the end the sleet had turned back into a proper snow. The result was a satisfactory surface for both skis and sleighs, and a sparkling, sun-drenched panorama of winter at its best.

Lucas heard Corrie take a deep breath, then sigh with pleasure. The tension between them eased, but sensual awareness still hummed like a low-voltage current never completely turned off.

He might as well abandon all efforts to resist her, he decided. He was powerfully attracted, not just to her physical beauty, but also to the person beneath the surface. He wasn't happy about the ghost thing, but he could pretend to go along with it, especially if it gave him an excuse to get to know Corrie more intimately. Perhaps, in time, she'd come to see that she'd imagined the whole thing.

And his father's testimony? Lucas dismissed that as an unfortunate side effect of the stroke. Pop was confused. Or else he'd meant Corrie herself when he spoke of a girl seeing a ghost.

"So what were you going to tell me about your progress with the phone calls?" Corrie asked.

Business first, Lucas reminded himself. Then pleasure. "We can't do much before Monday, except perhaps look at more family papers. Mom said she was going to leave some of them in your room while you were out. Also a folder with a family tree in it. She thought that might be useful for keeping names and dates straight."

"Monday?" She sounded disappointed.

"The town library is only open twenty hours a week and none of them are on weekends."

Corrie had found the scratchy wool blanket he kept under the seat and pulled it up over her lap, tucking it in around her legs and feet.

"Cold?"

"A little."

"That's part of the fun. To counteract it you have to dress warmly, bring along a heated brick for your feet, and cuddle close to the driver."

She sent him a quelling look and deliberately moved a few inches farther away from him. He chuckled and urged Lavinia to go faster.

He reminded her of a kid playing hookey from school, Corrie decided. As they continued their ride, he told her stories about the old days, when horses were the only means of transportation at the Sinclair House. He seemed to relish carrying on traditions, at least those from his own family's past. This wasn't the hotelier being "quaint." It was obvious to her that he drove this sleigh for his own pleasure . . . and hers.

The man was a charmer, all right, and she was in danger of falling under his spell. She knew it, yet she didn't try to fight becoming enthralled with him. She even felt a sense of disappointment when the sleigh rounded a turn and she spotted the hotel ahead of them again, looming up in the distance to mark the end of this peaceful, pleasant, quietly romantic interlude.

Against a backdrop formed by the White Mountains of New Hampshire, the white clapboard facade of the Sinclair House was dominated by two square five-story towers and the covered veranda that ran all the way around the hotel at the first-floor level. The sun was sinking low behind the building, throwing it into silhouette, bathing it in colored light. A magnificent sight, even if it was unwelcome.

The distance decreased rapidly as Lavinia trotted on. More details came into focus, and all at once, Corrie spotted something odd. She blinked hard, but the vision did not vanish. In one high window she saw a familiar face and form.

She stared at Adrienne, mesmerized, until she began to feel light-headed. Reality faded away, replaced by an overwhelming need. Obeying an urge too powerful to deny, Corrie turned in the seat, lifting her hands to frame Lucas's startled face. She forced his head down until his lips met her own, savoring the first brief contact, then returning to linger.

She lost herself in the deeper kiss that followed. As their tongues tangled in an ancient duel, she pressed herself close to him, hip to hip, breasts crushed against his broad chest. Her heart pounded faster, and her head swam.

She'd kissed men before, even kissed Lucas before, but never had it been such an overwhelming experience. Never had anything felt so right.

"Mmmm," Lucas moaned.

With the same sense she'd had upon waking in the middle of a dream, Corrie suddenly became aware of what she was doing. Horrified, she jerked away from Lucas, nearly tumbling backward off the high seat in her effort to escape.

What on earth had gotten into her? She'd never been the aggressive type.

Lucas reached for her, partly to catch her before she fell and partly to try to drag her back into his arms. "Don't stop now," he begged in a hoarse whisper.

But Lavinia chose that moment to take exception to the goings-on behind her. She tossed her head, setting the harness bells jangling. The sound brought them both to their senses.

"I'm s-sorry," Corrie stammered.

She'd grabbed the man by the face. She'd forced him to kiss her. Hot color climbed into her cheeks.

Lucas gave her a puzzled look before he gathered up the reins and headed the horse toward the hotel once more. As soon as he had Lavinia under control, he swung an arm around Corrie's shoulders, tucking her in tight against his side.

She allowed the liberty, but only so she could hide her face in the soft fabric of his jacket. "What must you think of me?" she whispered.

"That you're a beautiful, elegant, unexpected woman and that I'm a lucky man to have met you."

"What nonsense. I'm very ordinary."

"Not to me."

Flustered, she said nothing in response to that, but after a moment she tried again to explain away the behavior that had led to such a soul-shattering kiss. "I didn't intend to try to ravish you, Lucas. I—"

"You've got nothing to apologize for." His voice was so gruff and passionate, it sent chills down her spine. "If you hadn't decided to kiss me, sooner or later I'd have gotten around to kissing you again."

"You don't understand."

She wasn't the one who'd initiated their kiss. Some force stronger than she had literally pushed her into Lucas's arms.

Of its own volition, Corrie's gaze went back to the high window in the left tower. Adrienne was still there, staring down at her. And then, in the blink of an eye, she was gone.

"Are you cold?" Lucas asked when Corrie shivered.

"I'm fine."

Since her teeth were chattering audibly, she wasn't surprised when he didn't believe her.

"Relax, Corrie. I'm not offended. I'm flattered."

"I didn't mean to kiss you," she blurted out.

"The devil made you do it?" He was smiling at her as he said it, but one look at her face must have revealed what she was thinking. "Not that damned ghost business again?"

"Adrienne was watching us from a window," she said. "I don't know how she did it, but that kiss was her idea."

"That's ridiculous."

"Absurd," she agreed.

"You don't really believe she . . . possessed you?"

"Not exactly, but I do think power of suggestion was at work."

Lucas scowled fiercely. "Great. Listen, Corrie. I enjoyed kissing you. Hell, I even enjoyed the fact that you started it. And now you're trying to tell me that you didn't want to touch me at all?"

"I didn't say that."

"But you think it's a bad idea."

"Don't you?"

"I don't know what I think anymore."

Neither did Corrie. She'd kissed Lucas and had loved every second of the experience. But it hadn't been her idea to start with. That fact alone disturbed her, but the possibility that Adrienne had the power to compel her to act, overriding her self-control, was downright frightening.

What else was a ghost capable of orchestrating?

Lucas was no help. He appeared to have succumbed to the chemistry between them. He'd stopped trying to find reasons to resist temptation. And since he'd already warned her that he didn't intend to marry again, that left only one option, a fling with no commitment. Not exactly the stuff of a woman's romantic daydreams.

But what *did* she want? Was Lucas the Mr. Right

Rachel had suggested he was? In a way it was tempting to contemplate going along with Lucas's plan. Why not let him make love with her? Find out where this attraction would lead them.

Why not? Because she knew herself too well. She wasn't the sort of woman who could be intimate with a man and not want more. If he didn't want the same, she would be devastated. She was just asking for a broken heart if she let their relationship deepen.

As soon as the sleigh pulled up before the hotel entrance, where Lavinia's owner was waiting, Corrie hopped down from the seat. "Thanks for the lift," she said with patently false brightness.

Then, while Lucas was busy with horse and sleigh, she fled into the Sinclair House. It was more urgent now than ever that she unravel Adrienne's secrets. When she did, she could leave, hopefully with her heart still intact.

In this building, somewhere, a ghost was waiting for her.

Out of the frying pan and into the fire, Corrie thought as she passed through the lobby and entered the old-fashioned elevator.

Or was it the other way around?

Lucas had no intention of pursuing an unwilling woman. He was also having second thoughts about his interest in one particular woman who claimed to be the victim of a matchmaking ghost powerful enough to thrust her into his arms. He told himself he was relieved when Corrie and Rachel chose to leave the hotel for dinner Saturday evening.

But the woman haunting his dreams that night was not Adrienne Sinclair. By Sunday morning, Lucas gave in to the inevitable. He didn't want to stay away from Corrie. When he spotted her from a hotel window, walking alone along a flagstone path, he grabbed his coat and went out to join her.

"Nice day for a stroll," he remarked as he fell into step beside her.

"I thought I'd see where this path led," she said in a neutral voice.

"Do you mind company?"

"No. Actually, I was going to look for you later."

"Seen Adrienne again?"

"No, worse luck. Not a trace. I didn't even dream about her. But talking to your mother about gimmicks must have triggered my subconscious because all night long I kept coming up with possibilities for bringing new business to the hotel. I must have turned on the bedside lamp half a dozen times to write ideas down." She shot a sheepish smile his way. "I didn't want to risk forgetting anything."

"What sort of ideas?" Lucas supposed he should be pleased she was taking an interest in the hotel's welfare, but he couldn't help thinking that there was a secluded spot up ahead where he might manage to interest her in more personal matters.

"Murder mystery weekends."

The suggestion brought him up short and jerked his thoughts away from romance. "You aren't suggesting a conference, I hope." He gave her a brief recap of the plans for the Cozies Unlimited gathering.

"Small conferences aren't a bad idea, but they have to be well planned. Use all available space for meeting rooms, banquets and so forth, so that the hotel is assured of making a profit. But I was actually thinking of even smaller groups, no more than twenty or thirty people at a time. There are several ways to handle murder mystery weekends. Sometimes hired actors perform the bulk of the presentation, with paying guests taking on limited roles. Sometimes it's almost entirely an amateur affair. People get together to role-play. These events can be quite successful if they're managed right."

"And disastrous in inept hands."

"There is that."

Imaginative and practical at the same time. Lucas realized that he liked that combination in a woman. It occurred to him, too, that he'd stopped comparing Corrie to Dina. The two women were nothing alike.

Dina had been focused on the bottom line and didn't have a fanciful bone in her voluptuous body. More crucially, she'd also lacked family feeling. She'd coldheartedly "forgotten" to tell him when his father had called to ask for Lucas's help. Embroiled in the trouble Stanley Kelvin's embezzlement had caused, the Sinclair House had almost been lost as a result. Lucas had discovered his wife's deception just in time.

Sensing his dark thoughts, though she misunderstood their cause, Corrie cocked her head sideways. "If you don't like that idea, you might consider trying to attract historical reenactment buffs. There does seem to be a great deal of information available on what the hotel was like in Adrienne's day."

Some of it hadn't changed much since then, he thought. Had the first Lucas courted his Adrienne in this grove of pines? It had been a popular spot to take tea on a summer afternoon. Men in coats and ties and women in flowered hats would gather to socialize. Lucas thought he liked it better in winter, when he could be alone with the woman beside him.

Corrie gave him an encouraging smile as they walked on, but when she spoke it was to ask about Adrienne again. Damn ghost!

"Your mother said Adrienne was responsible for installing tennis courts and a tenpin bowling alley and the golf course, and that she had a specially dug and stocked fishpond put in near the springhouse. Is that it just ahead?"

"Yes. It was originally dug as a fishpond, then expanded into a swimming hole." They approached the ice-covered pond. "Adrienne made rowboats available for those who wanted to while away their vacation with a pole and a can of worms. Before people started to insist on heated and chlorinated water and pool filters, swimming in lakes and ponds, man-made or otherwise, was a popular sport."

"You don't sound too fond of modern swimming pools, and yet you have one."

"A recent addition. Pop's idea." Lucas still found it astonishing that so many of their winter guests were fool enough to strip down to skimpy swimwear and frolic in water surrounded by snow. "Nuts," he commented under his breath.

"If being crazy is the criteria for swimming outdoors in the dead of winter, then by rights I should be on my way to the hotel gift shop right this minute to buy myself a suit."

Lucas enjoyed a brief, tantalizing image of Corrie in a bikini before he responded to the more telling part of her remark. "For the record, I don't think you're crazy." Neither were the folks who used the Sinclair House pool. They slipped into heated water through an indoor tunnel, descending steps at one end of the locker room to swim out into the pool itself. As long as they stayed in the water while they were out of doors, they remained comfortably warm.

"It occurs to me that I may be having a nervous breakdown," Corrie confessed.

Lucas felt a stab of concern. The idea of Corrie suffering was upsetting.

"What if there is no ghost?" she continued. "What if she's a figment of my imagination? Let's face it, paranormal experiences just don't happen to ordinary people."

He refrained from sharing his first response to that little speech, that she was far from ordinary. Instead he answered her question with one of his own. "Why would you be having a breakdown?"

"My mother died last year at Christmastime," she said as they circled the pond. "Maybe I'm having a delayed reaction." The explanation came so reluctantly that Lucas suspected she regretted broaching the subject.

"Is your father still living?" he asked.

"Oh, yes." Now she sounded bitter. He'd wondered why she wasn't spending the holiday with her family. He was still curious, but a close inspection of her closed expression made him decide to shift the conversation back to his own family.

"I'm curious about something," he said. "A little while ago, when I asked if you'd seen Adrienne again, you said, 'No, worse luck.' If you were so anxious to encounter her, why did you avoid the hotel dining room last night?"

Unwilling to look at him, Corrie kept walking, eyes on the path ahead. By now they were going back the way they'd come and were once more passing the pine grove.

"Call it an approach/avoidance problem," she said after a moment. "I did want to confront Adrienne after our sleigh ride, but as suppertime approached I realized that I didn't want to risk a repeat performance of what happened Christmas night. I can take only so much public humiliation. No one else would have seen her if she'd appeared in the dining room a second time, but I'd have been desperately trying to find someone who could. I'd have ended up making a fool of myself, and I just couldn't face having that happen."

"Was it simply that you didn't want to be embarrassed," Lucas asked, "or also that you preferred not to see me again just then?" He held his breath waiting for her answer.

"Maybe a little of both," she admitted. "This is a very weird situation, Lucas. I don't know what to think. About anything."

Weird. She had that right. He didn't like to think too carefully about why he was out there with her instead of in his office, working.

With a sigh and a shrug, she finally glanced up at him. "Maybe I *am* having a mental breakdown. Maybe there *is* no ghost."

"But, Corrie," he said, unable to resist, "if there is no Adrienne, wouldn't that mean it was all your own idea to kiss me?"

Color flooded into her face as she came to an abrupt halt. She swallowed hard. "I guess if my imagination has run wild since I arrived at the Sinclair House, my libido could have too. But that's not my usual style, believe me."

He smiled and yielded to the impulse to lean down and gently kiss the healing gash on her forehead. Then he took her arm and resumed walking.

"Stress does do funny things to a person," he said, "but I'd like to think what we feel for each other when we're together isn't the result of anything more mysterious than a strong mutual attraction. I like you, Corrie. In fact, I'd like to—"

He broke off, perplexed, when he realized her gaze was fixed on the hotel ahead.

As he looked into her stricken face, he saw her close her eyes, then open them again. At once she drew in a sharp breath. Then she jerked away from him and began to run toward the hotel.

He caught up with her just as she was climbing the wide stairs to the veranda. "Corrie?" He grabbed her by the forearms, turning her to face him and giving her a little shake to get her attention.

When her expression remained as blank as a clean slate, Lucas didn't hesitate. Heedless of curious stares, he picked Corrie up and carried her into the hotel.

As soon as the warm air in the lobby hit her, she snapped out of her trance. Docility vanished as she started to struggle. "What are you doing? Put me down."

He ignored her rancorous words and strode toward the bank of elevators. "Did you know," he said, maintaining a conversational tone and pausing to smile politely at passing hotel guests, "that this elevator operates in the same shaft used by the first one ever installed in the hotel, way back in Adrienne's day?"

"Do tell." Nettled, Corrie fixed her gaze on the panel, watching the slow-moving floor indicator drift toward the *L*.

"It was considered quite innovative back in 1883. Advertised as very safe, being hydraulic. A cable opened a valve that allowed water to enter the shaft and that forced the elevator to ascend. To descend, the water was slowly released to lower the elevator. The only problem came when they wanted to hold it steady at one floor. It tended to drift."

The elevator stopped on the second floor.

"It could do with a little drift right now." Corrie sounded miffed. "And you can put me down anytime."

He opened his mouth, then closed it again. He'd

been babbling like some fool tour guide in an absurd attempt to make it seem that carrying a woman through the lobby was a normal, everyday thing to do.

For the first time in his life, Lucas Sinclair of the Sinclair House wished all the hotel's paying guests would simply disappear. He wanted to be alone with Corrie. He wanted to tell her he cared about her, that he was worried about her.

And he wanted to find out what on earth, or off it, had caused her to behave as she had just now. But he had the feeling he already knew the answer to that question.

Maybe babbling wasn't such a bad way to go.

"Electric communicators were installed at about the same time," he said brightly as another couple passed by and gave them a curious look. "Those were the first intercoms. We also had an electric light plant in use by 1881. Electric lights were installed in all the public rooms and in the bathrooms."

"I've read the literature," Corrie informed him, and paraphrased Adrienne's text to prove it: "Standard furnishings included sitz baths, showers, pink marble washbasins, and vases of peacock feathers. The baths were vented with electric exhaust fans guaranteed to eliminate 'noxious fumes.'"

At last the elevator door opened. Lucas stepped inside, still carrying Corrie. Only when they were safely enclosed by the cage did he let her go. As her legs slid languidly down his body, he shifted the arm that had been supporting her lower back and curved it around her shoulders. He wasn't about to let go of her completely, not until they were safe in her room.

Corrie continued to look a trifle dazed, and she offered no word of protest when he ushered her out of the elevator on the third floor and steered her down the hall toward her door. Rachel came out of her room across the hall as he was using his master key to unlock Corrie's door. One look at her friend's pale face had her rushing to join them.

Inside, Corrie discarded her coat, revealing a pale blue sweater that matched her eyes, and drifted to the window. Lucas knew she was staring down at the roof of the veranda.

"Have you seen Adrienne again?" Rachel demanded.

Lucas started to say yes, but Corrie spoke before he could get the word out. "It wasn't even the same century."

"What the hell?" He'd been prepared, more or less, to cope with another Adrienne sighting. This unexpected announcement threw him a curve.

"There was a peculiar smell in the air," Corrie said. "Smoke, I think. In fact, I'm pretty sure it must have been, and the year had to be 1947." Her voice started to shake. "During the wildfires."

Lucas almost lost his temper then. What kind of credulous fool did she take him for?

"Start at the beginning," Rachel cut in. "What exactly did you see?"

Corrie shook her head, as if to clear her thoughts, and set a cloud of soft brown hair swirling. Lucas swallowed hard. He didn't like this one bit, but he might as well let her talk. He braced himself for more unwelcome revelations.

"Lucas and I were taking a walk and I had just glanced toward the hotel," Corrie said, "when suddenly the daylight seemed to dim. Then the snow-covered ground and the bare branches faded away. In their place was a rolling lawn just beginning to turn brown. Trees still had the last colorful leaves of autumn clinging to their branches. I was standing on a gravel path, not flagstones." She frowned, trying to recall details. "It was bordered by a low-growing plant. Hyssop, I think."

Startled, Lucas almost spoke. How could she possibly know that? He only knew because the alterations had been made when he was a teenager and he remembered the gardener complaining. Old Ernest hadn't liked change.

Corrie continued to stare out the window. Lucas couldn't make out her expression, but the timbre of her voice told him she believed every word she said. "I saw three people posed on the veranda, waiting while a photographer took their picture."

Of course, Lucas thought. That explained it. She'd seen a picture of the old path to the pond. That's how she knew about the hyssop and the gravel.

"They were on vacation," Corrie continued, "but they were going to cut their stay short because of the increasing fire danger in the area."

"Who were these people?" Lucas asked.

"A girl and her parents."

"Girl? The girl who supposedly saw Adrienne's ghost?"

"I think so." Corrie finally turned and met his eyes. Her face was ashen, her expression fearful. "Lucas, I recognized her. I've seen the photograph they had taken that day."

He knew in advance he wouldn't like her reply, but he asked anyway. "Who was she?"

Corrie drew in a deep, strengthening breath before blurting out her answer. "That girl was my mother."

SEVEN

Lucas didn't believe her.

Corrie could see it in his eyes the moment she made her startling announcement.

To his credit, he didn't immediately turn his back and stalk out of her room, though she thought he might secretly want to. He seemed too concerned about her emotional state to follow through on the impulse. The realization that he cared warmed her heart even as it complicated her feelings.

"Don't humor me," she warned as he started to speak. "I know it sounds preposterous. I wouldn't believe me if I told myself such a story."

"Corrie, I . . ." His voice trailed off, and he raked his fingers through his hair. "I don't know what to say. Or what to believe."

"Just don't suggest a shrink. This time I *know* what I saw."

Rachel cleared her throat. "Y'know, you're overlooking something here. Remember when I first suggested we come to the Sinclair House? You got an odd look on your face and then you agreed without a bit of argument. Why?"

"I don't know. Maybe the name had a familiar ring to it." A positive one, she remembered. She'd jumped at the invitation because it *felt* right. She'd thought at the time that she was simply glad of any excuse to be hundreds of miles away from her father and brothers at Christmas, but what if it had been more than that?

"Could your mother have stayed here and talked about the place?" Rachel went on. "Maybe even mentioned the portrait of Adrienne? Kids tuck the most amazing things away in their subconscious, and you always did have a wild imagination."

"You're saying I dreamed all this up from stories I heard about my mother's visit to the Sinclair House when she was a child? But I don't remember being told any!"

Relief plain in his voice, Lucas spoke. "We have old registers. I can check for her name."

"Alice Todd. Her parents were Mary and David Todd."

Corrie worried her lower lip with her teeth. Something wasn't right about this explanation. Oh, she'd like it to be true, but it wouldn't account for everything. It didn't account for Horatio.

"I'd like to be alone now," she said abruptly. "I need to think."

As soon as Lucas and Rachel had left, Corrie headed for the phone. On Christmas Day, when she had called to tell her father where she was spending the holidays, he'd said he'd heard of the Sinclair House.

Now she needed to know where and when.

That it probably had something to do with her mother made phoning him awkward. Since her death they'd both avoided mention of Alice Ballantyne. The pain of losing her still ran deep. So did Corrie's resentment. And her sense of guilt.

With a troubled mind, she dialed the number. She nearly hung up before it rang.

Ten minutes later she was no less troubled, but she did have a few answers. Her mother had stayed at the Sinclair House when she was barely in her teens. That fit the date 1947. She hadn't spoken of the visit often, Corrie's father had said, but she had told him that it had been a "unique" experience. She'd suggested spending a vacation there once, but they'd decided it would be too expensive.

"I'm sorry now we didn't splurge," Donald Ballantyne had said. He sounded remorseful, as if he wished he'd recognized how much such a trip would have meant to his wife. "I thought that's why you picked the place. Because she'd talked about it to you."

She never had. Not that Corrie could recall. And wouldn't she remember if her mother had mentioned seeing a ghost when she was young?

"Corrie?" Her father sounded worried.

"Sorry, Daddy. I was trying to piece a few things together. Do you ever remember seeing an old photograph of Mother and her parents? One that might have been taken here at the Sinclair House?"

"Doesn't ring a bell, but I could look through Alice's belongings if you want." He sighed deeply. "We need to go through those boxes in the attic. Get some closure."

Corrie didn't want to hear this. "Daddy, I—"

"Your sisters-in-law had a few things to say on Christmas Day about the way your brothers and I expected you to take your mother's place. Opened our eyes a bit." He hesitated, then said, "I grieve every day for my Alice, and not just because she left me behind to fend for myself, either. I loved your mother, Corrie. I'd have died in her place if I could have."

An uneasy silence ensued. Corrie didn't want to talk about her mother, except in the limited context of Alice's long-ago visit to the Sinclair House. Not now. And not over the phone.

"I have to go, Daddy. I'll be back home next weekend."

She broke the connection quickly, then felt guilty for all but hanging up on him.

Soon, she promised herself. Soon she'd gather the courage to tell her father how she felt, why she was having so much trouble forgiving him for her mother's death. Why she was having so much trouble forgiving herself.

That night Corrie tossed restlessly, unsuccessfully courting sleep until she finally abandoned the effort and scooted toward the head of the bed, plumped the pillows behind her, and turned on the lamp on the bedside table. She'd been trying for days to read the novel that lay there. Tonight she vowed she'd succeed.

Then she remembered the red file folder Joyce had sent to the room along with two cartons full of photographs and memorabilia from Adrienne's era. Corrie had gone through the boxes but found nothing to give her any hint of the ghost's purpose in returning from the dead.

The folder contained the Sinclair family tree. She had only glanced at it the previous day; now it drew her. She got out of bed, put on her robe, and curled up in the room's overstuffed chair to study it more closely.

The file contained only one sheet of paper, a handdrawn chart that included both the Meads and the Sinclairs. Joyce had annotated it here and there to make the connections clearer.

Micah Mead, father to Adrienne and Horatio, was at the top of the page. Corrie saw that Horatio had been more than a decade older than his sister. According to Joyce's notes, Micah and Horatio had opened the Phoenix Inn in 1868. The next year Adrienne had married their chief competitor, Lucas Sinclair.

Skipping to the next generation, Corrie's gaze immediately fell on the name Jonathan Mead. She remembered that she'd dreamed about him. Afterward, the dream had faded, and so too had her curiosity about him. She'd never even thought to ask anyone who he was.

According to the family tree, he was Horatio's son, born in 1875. She glanced back at the line that showed the date of his parents' marriage. Also 1875. No months or days were written on the chart, but it didn't look to Corrie as if the boy was legally a bastard. That left the other sense of the word, as she'd thought when she first woke up.

What did he have to do with anything? She found no answer, so she read on, skimming the rest of the chart. Jonathan had had a younger sister named Marguerite, born in 1878. According to Joyce's dates, Marguerite had died when she was only eighteen. Corrie shook her head. So many people had lived such short lives in those days.

For a moment her attention wandered to the other side of the chart. Joyce had mentioned that the Sinclair men were known for their longevity, and Corrie saw at once that this was true. There was Justus Sinclair, Hugh's father, who'd lived to be ninety. And his father and grandfather before him had achieved similar life spans.

The women hadn't fared as well. Corrie suspected that they'd been worn out by hard work, since there didn't seem to be evidence of excessive childbearing. In each generation of Sinclairs there was just one child, a son to carry on the Sinclair name and tradition. A son to run the Sinclair House.

The Mead side of the chart wasn't much more prolific. Erastus Mead, Jonathan's son, had produced one daughter, another Marguerite, who had become Stanley Kelvin's mother. Joyce had put the nickname Rita in parentheses after Marguerite.

There were no answers on this chart, Corrie decided, though she continued to stare at it until her eyelids grew heavy. Before she realized what was happening, she fell asleep in the chair.

She woke with a start. Again.

She'd been dreaming. Again.

And again she could not remember much of the dream, except that Marguerite, Horatio's daughter, had been in it. Adrienne and her niece had been discussing the paltry wages paid to hotel workers in the 1890s.

A glimmer of a memory from her own childhood surfaced in Corrie's mind. Her mother's mother, Mary Hanover Todd, had been the one to tell Corrie and her brothers about her own mother, Daisy. As a young woman, Daisy Hanover had done what Grandma Mary called "slave labor" in the kitchen of a resort hotel in the Catskills. She'd stood, hour after hour, washing dishes until her hands were nothing but red blotches and peeling skin.

As Rachel had recently reminded her, the story had a romantic and happy ending. At least Corrie had thought so when she was young. In their free time, the hotel employees had been permitted to socialize with one another. A young man who worked at the resort had courted Daisy, spending hours with her in one of the huge hammocks strung between giant trees on the hotel grounds. Eventually, he'd married her and taken her away from the drudgery of working for strangers.

Corrie reached for the family tree that had fallen to the floor while she slept. There was Marguerite, all right, the young woman who had died at eighteen. Corrie wondered if she'd lived long enough to fall in love. How sad it was to have had such a short life, and to have that life reduced to two lines on a chart.

Sighing, Corrie stood and stretched. It was almost dawn. She might as well stay up. And today, she remembered, was Monday, when she'd planned to go digging for information about Adrienne at the local library.

Was it worth the effort? What if there wasn't any ghost? What if it had all been her imagination?

If she had any common sense, she thought, she'd abandon this fruitless quest and concentrate on finding out where her attraction to Lucas Sinclair might lead. One thing was certain. All this paranormal business was doing more to drive them apart than bring them together.

Focus on the possible, she lectured herself. Forget romance. Stop remembering how right it had felt to kiss Lucas Sinclair.

She had a connection to Adrienne in her mother's visit to the hotel. At the moment that only produced more questions, but Corrie thought she might be able to discover something at the library about events in 1947, something that would give her a clue.

Having a specific goal gave a lightness to her steps as she headed for the bathroom and a long, leisurely soak in the tub. It was a new day. She'd make a fresh start. She'd figure this out.

And she'd find a way to deal with her irrational fondness for Lucas Sinclair too.

Adrienne muttered an unladylike curse.

If only she could gather strength enough to project everything into Corrie Ballantyne's consciousness at once. This hit-or-miss, stop-and-start communication frustrated her no end.

Corrie kept missing essential bits of information.

Try as she might, Adrienne could not control what got through and what didn't. Just the effort was exhausting.

Sighing as deeply as Corrie had, Adrienne worried she might not succeed, after all. Would she ever resolve the guilt she'd felt during the last year of her own lifetime and after?

For a hundred years she'd been separated from the man she loved. Wasn't that enough to expiate a sin of omission?

Corrie was in the car, about to leave the hotel for the public library, when Lucas slid into the passenger seat. "No sense taking two vehicles," he said, "though we could walk."

"Walking seems to get me into trouble," she informed him.

So did riding in a sleigh, but Lucas had the good sense not to remind her of that. Neither did he bring up his own skepticism about her "sightings." Instead he gave her directions to the library, then played the quintessential gentleman when they reached their destination by taking her elbow to squire her through the heavy oak doors that guarded its contents.

Any excuse to touch her, he thought, grinning wryly. Did she have the slightest idea how she affected him? Probably not. And probably just as well. He had to laugh at himself now for thinking, on the night they first met, that he could resist her. Even her strange aberration, the fact that she thought she saw things that weren't there, wasn't enough to keep him away from her.

The dour-faced doyenne of the Waycross Springs Public Library was waiting for them just inside. "Ah, Mrs. Prentiss," Lucas greeted her. "You're looking well this morning."

"Thank you, dear boy." She poked self-consciously at a strand of iron-gray hair that had tumbled across her forehead, but her attention was fixed on Corrie. "Who have we here?"

"This is Corrie Ballantyne, a guest at the hotel and a friend of the family. She's interested in local history."

"Family come from here?" Mrs. Prentiss asked.

"Not that I know of," Corrie answered.

The inquisition might have gone on for some time had Lucas not reminded Mrs. Prentiss she'd promised to direct them to any documents that concerned either Adrienne or her brother Horatio.

Corrie also asked for newspapers from 1947.

A short time later, she was ensconced at one of the long worktables in the reading room, surrounded by yellowing, slightly musty-smelling pages. Decades behind the times, this small, underfunded local facility couldn't afford microfilm. Fortunately, the *Waycross Springs Gazette* was a weekly and rarely more than eight pages long.

Seated at her side, Lucas paused in his own research to watch her scan issues from October of 1947. What was it that drew him to her? She had a quiet dignity that was appealing, yet he knew she was not at all placid when dealing with something she cared about. Perhaps that was it. He wanted to delve beneath the surface, to tap into the passion she tried to keep hidden. He wanted to *be* the something she cared passionately about.

He was getting fanciful. As bad as Corrie herself. How could he let himself fall for a woman who thought she saw ghosts? A woman who wasn't able to tell reality from illusion?

She looked up just then and smiled at him, and his heart raced. Whatever was between them, it was powerful. And it wasn't likely to go away anytime soon.

"This isn't helping, but it's kind of fascinating," she said, gesturing to the page spread out in front of her. "In 1947 I could have bought a washing machine and had it delivered for one hundred and twenty-nine dollars and fifty cents."

Lucas glanced at the other ads on the page. Quart bottles of ginger ale, root beer, sarsaparilla, and Moxie were offered for fifteen cents each, plus deposit. Swimsuits for toddlers sold for fifty-nine cents and up.

Reaching past Corrie, he picked up the next issue,

dated October 17th. The middle of the front page carried a story about closing down the woods due to fire danger. At the movie theater Joan Crawford was starring in *Possessed*, a double feature with *Jesse James Rides Again*.

Intensely aware of Corrie watching him, he read about a barn destroyed in a flash fire. Volunteers had fought the blaze with Indian pumps and brooms, but their efforts had been severely limited by lack of water. Finally some had been brought in using maple syrup tanks, but not before nine cows, a pair of horses, a bull, and a calf had perished.

Not a single mention was made of a ghost having appeared to a guest at the Sinclair House.

"Oh, well. It was always a long shot," Corrie murmured.

She looked so forlorn that he wanted to take her in his arms and comfort her. Hell, he wanted to do far more than that! He was trying to think of some way to get past the barrier of her belief in the supernatural when Mrs. Prentiss appeared at his elbow.

"Lucas," she said. "There's a phone call for you."

Corrie watched him leave with a sense of growing dismay. She'd been so enthralled by his presence at her side that she hadn't even heard the telephone ringing.

Why did the man have to be so attractive? She wanted to keep the intellectual puzzle, the mysteries of Adrienne and of her own mother's apparent sighting, separate from how she felt about Lucas. She couldn't do it. He was inextricably bound up in what had gone before and, somehow, so was she.

Frowning, Corrie tried to sort out what that meant. What was the connection? Why did Adrienne only appear to women in Corrie's family?

Or was that assumption wrong? Apparently her own mother hadn't told anyone she'd seen a ghost, except Hugh Sinclair and maybe her parents. Perhaps dozens of other people over the years had seen Adrienne but had kept quiet about it, fearing ridicule or simply refusing to believe the evidence of their own eyes.

A sudden conviction came to Corrie that the answers weren't there at the library. They were at the hotel. Somehow she had to find a better way to communicate with the Sinclair House ghost.

"I have to go back," Lucas announced as he returned. "Minor emergency at the hotel."

"I'll drive you," she said.

"You don't want to stay here? You haven't even started on the material from the 1890s."

"It's not going to help."

He started to object, then seemed to think better of it. "Whatever you say, Corrie."

Lucas didn't utter another word until they reached the hotel, and Corrie berated herself the whole way. She'd mishandled Lucas from the start. She should have found a better way to tell him about seeing Adrienne in the dining room on Christmas night. But no. She'd just blurted it out. How could she blame him for being so skeptical? It was a tribute to his character that he'd humored her to the extent he had. As far as she knew, he hadn't even considered sending for the little men in the white coats.

They turned the car over to a valet and entered the lobby together. Corrie expected Lucas to go straight to the registration desk, where Joyce was waiting to consult with him over whatever problem had come up. Instead he drew her aside, behind one of the huge pillars. There was an illusion of privacy there, without the intimacy of being together in his office or her room.

"Here's the thing, Corrie. Between now and New Year's Eve I'm going to be right out straight with hotel business, but I'd like it very much if you'd promise me two things."

"What things?"

"First, that if you have any more sightings you'll let me know right away. That goes for sudden insights too. Or if anything upsets you for any reason. I want to know, okay?"

"Okay. Was that one promise or two?"

"One. You and I also have some unfinished personal business to take care of."

"Personal?" He was standing much too close. She couldn't think clearly. Did he mean what she hoped he did?

"Yes, personal. As in nothing whatsoever to do with the supernatural."

"And this second promise you wanted from me?"

He started to say something but caught himself. "Save me a dance New Year's Eve?"

"Sure," she agreed, fighting a sense of chagrin, "if you tell me what you originally planned to ask me."

He glanced toward the registration desk and shifted his weight. "I don't have time to beat around the bush," he said bluntly. "I was going to ask you to spend the evening with me."

"And you decided that wasn't wise?"

"I decided that wouldn't be fair to you. I'll be working."

She suspected he wasn't telling her the whole truth, even now, but she didn't choose to pursue the issue. She was too unsure of how she felt about him. Her resolve not to get any more involved with him seemed to weaken every time she was in his company.

"You're only asking for the evening, not the night," she said in what she hoped was a light tone of voice.

"All right, then. Let's spend the evening together."

"Agreed. The whole evening."

Trouble was, she wanted to spend the whole night with Lucas Sinclair too.

He gave a wry chuckle. "You look as if you're already reconsidering."

"I've said I want to spend the evening with you." Knowing she sounded testy, she tried to soften her tone. "As Rachel would say, what could it hurt?"

"I don't think I'm going to answer that."

Catching her off guard, he bent forward and brushed his lips across her mouth. He retreated before she could say a word.

She watched him stop to speak with Joyce, then go

on into his office. It wasn't until he was out of sight that Corrie realized Joyce must have witnessed their kiss. Lucas's mother was positively beaming.

"Oh, great," Corrie muttered. "Nothing like encouraging the matchmakers."

Still, she didn't feel quite as irritated as she would have a few days earlier. She started to return to her room, then did a Columbo-style turn and advanced on the registration desk.

"Joyce, have you got a minute? I have a question."

"Of course, my dear. What is it?"

"It's about the 1947 fires."

"Lucas told me you saw your mother. I looked in the old hotel registers, but there are no entries for October of 1947. The hotel closed for the season in September."

"That's not possible."

"I'm sorry, Corrie, but it is. I should have realized sooner. Till we winterized, only a few exceptions were made. A visiting dignitary, perhaps, who didn't mind that the only heat came from the fireplace in the room."

"I don't suppose you remember any visitors that year. I know you must have been a young child yourself, but—"

"I wasn't here yet."

"I'm sorry. I didn't mean—"

"Your guess at my age is accurate enough," Joyce said, amusement making her eyes twinkle, "but I didn't move to Maine until after Lucas was born. I met and married Hugh in Colorado. We didn't live in

Waycross Springs until Hugh's father asked him to come back and help him run the place."

"But you know so much of the history."

"That should have been your first hint," Joyce said with a laugh. "It's almost always the outsider who wants to belong who goes in for ancestor worship in a big way."

Corrie was glad the phone rang just then, demanding Joyce's attention. She needed a little time alone to absorb this new thought. It was true, she realized. People tended to neglect their own family heritage, to take whatever they'd been told for granted.

What did she really know about her mother, Alice Todd Ballantyne? Or her grandmother, Mary Hanover Todd? And she couldn't even remember Great-grandmother Daisy Hanover's maiden name.

Resolved to remedy her own ignorance after she returned home, Corrie set about implementing a new plan to link with Adrienne. She went into the dining room, even though it was too early for lunch, and sat at the table from which she'd seen Adrienne and her Lucas on Christmas night.

She sat there for a very long time.

Absolutely nothing happened.

EIGHT

That evening Lucas found Corrie alone at a table in the dining room. "May I join you?" he asked.

"Please. Rachel has a date tonight with someone she met skiing."

Lucas sat and signaled the waiter. "I'm afraid I'll have to eat and run."

"At least you're not just wolfing down a sandwich at your desk."

He grinned. "You sound like my mother. Nag. Nag. Nag."

"You deserve it if you work yourself too hard."

After they gave their orders, Lucas broached the subject he wanted to get out of the way first. "Any further signs of Adrienne or your mother?" That Corrie hadn't contacted him all afternoon probably meant she hadn't seen Adrienne again. He'd caught himself once or twice wishing she had, if only because that would have given her an excuse to stop by his office.

"No," she said. "And I've spent a good deal of time right here today, hoping she'd show up. That she hasn't is beginning to make me nervous. I keep wondering if the haunting has stopped and I'm supposed to figure things out from the clues I've already gotten. If so, we're in trouble. I've tried, but I come up blank. I just don't have enough information."

"Let's not discuss ghosts anymore this evening," he suggested after their salads were served. "Surely there are other things we can talk about."

They discussed favorite books until the entrées arrived.

"What now?" she asked, smiling. "The weather?"

"You?"

"I'm a pretty boring subject."

"Not to me. You could tell me about your family."

"There's not much to say." Her tone of voice made him certain there was a great deal more he wanted to learn about them.

Lucas discovered he wasn't tasting a bite of what was probably a delicious filet mignon. All his senses were occupied with Corrie. The delicate scent of her perfume teased him from across the table. As she lifted a dainty morsel to her mouth, his own mouth watered at the thought of touching those lips with his.

"You do *have* a family, right?"

She pretended to be fascinated by the seafood platter in front of her. "Yes, of course I do."

"You said the other day that your mother died last year at Christmas. It's never easy to lose a loved one, but it must be especially hard when the loss is associated with a holiday."

"She died right *after* Christmas." Corrie's bitterness underscored every word. She speared a scallop with unnecessary force, nearly sending it skittering off her plate.

"I'm sorry," he murmured. "If you'd rather not talk about it, I'll drop the subject."

But he'd gotten her started now. She stopped eating and fixed him with a level gaze. "She knocked herself out making everything perfect for my father and my brothers and their families. She put off going to a doctor about her own health. Put it off until it was too late to do anything. She died of cancer, cancer that would have been operable if they'd only caught it in time."

"I'm sorry," he said again. This time he meant it.

"I couldn't face being with them this year."

Them. Her father and brothers. "You blame them?"

"Yes, I do. Why didn't my father, who claimed to love her, notice that she was in pain? Why didn't he insist she take care of herself?" Corrie sighed and picked up her fork once more to toy with the food on her plate. "I blame myself too. I wasn't home a lot, but I could see she was too pale, too thin. It just never occurred to me that there could be something seriously wrong with her. She was my mother. She was supposed to be there for me. Always."

"Perhaps that's what your father thought as well."

"He's too self-centered. So are my brothers. As

long as she was there to slave for them, they hardly noticed she was alive."

Her words shocked him. Corrie certainly had a different view of family and family commitments than he did. Or was it just that she was still hurting, still recovering from the loss of her mother?

"Family is too important to let an estrangement grow," he said. "Have you considered how much you'll regret this rift if it continues?"

"I didn't start it." She resumed eating, a clear hint that they'd said enough on this subject, but Lucas couldn't let it go.

"If they're as self-centered as you say, then it's up to you to mend fences."

"Oh, they'd like that. Another woman to take advantage of. Thank you, no." Her hand was trembling slightly as she reached for her wineglass.

"Maybe they're feeling just as guilty about neglecting your mother as you are. Maybe if you talk to each other—"

"They don't talk. They lecture. Or try to boss me around." She sipped, and sipped again, then carefully put the glass down.

Lucas caught her hand before she could move it from the top of the table. Her head jerked up, her eyes startled as her gaze collided with his.

"And if your father has, say, a stroke, when you're still estranged? If he dies before you've reconciled?"

The stricken look on her face was enough to tell him he'd gotten through to her, even though her words continued to deny it. "This isn't any of your business, Lucas."

"You're right. It isn't. But I find I care about you, Corrie, and it's obvious this is tearing you apart."

With another sigh, she eased her hand out of his grip and off the table. He suspected both hands were now tightly clenched in her lap, but her voice sounded calm enough, almost matter-of-fact. "My family isn't like yours, Lucas. And sometimes a person has to choose personal desires over what the family wants. Haven't you ever been in that situation?"

"Oh, yes." Now he was the one who sounded bitter, the one who looked away. "I had to choose between my family and my wife."

He didn't need to tell her who had won.

They stuck with neutral topics for the remainder of the meal.

The moment Corrie entered her room that evening, she sensed another presence. Adrienne was waiting for her by the window. As soon as Corrie appeared, Adrienne walked to the door Corrie was still holding open, beckoning for her to follow.

"Well, finally. Some action."

Corrie was only sorry Lucas wasn't with her, but she was too afraid Adrienne would vanish again to stop and phone the front desk, where he would be until midnight. Besides, they hadn't parted on the best of terms. After they finally stopped talking about families, conversation had become rather stilted. He'd seemed almost relieved to have the excuse of getting back to work.

Without hesitation, Adrienne led the way into an unused portion of the hotel, where the scent of furniture polish and floor wax was overlaid with the heaviness of a thick coat of dust. It was also very cold in this unheated area. All of the radiators had been drained to save energy and keep the pipes from freezing.

Corrie wrapped her arms about herself for warmth, glad she was wearing a heavy sweater but wishing she'd thought to grab her coat.

Low-wattage bulbs lit the hallways and stairs, and Corrie would soon have been lost in the maze if not for Adrienne leading the way. Other than the two of them, not a creature was stirring, not even the legendary mouse. An eerie atmosphere compounded the emptiness. Corrie was relieved when Adrienne finally reached her goal and passed over the threshold of one particular room. From the inside, Corrie heard a distinct clicking sound as the door was unlocked.

The first thing Corrie did after opening it was feel for the light switch. She wasn't at all sure she'd have gone in if bright illumination hadn't immediately flooded the room. Dustcovers protected the oversize furnishings, but a quick peek told her that the pieces were antiques, much like the ornate oak bed and armoire in her own room.

Cautiously, she looked around, trying to guess why the ghost had brought her to this particular room. "What am I supposed to find?" she asked aloud.

She didn't really expect an answer, at least not a

verbal one, but neither was she prepared for what abruptly appeared in front of her eyes. Adrienne vanished. So did the dustcovers. There were now four people in the room. One man looked like Lucas. The others were Corrie's mother and grandparents.

Suddenly she knew this was Hugh, not Lucas. On closer inspection he looked younger than Lucas was now. And so real that she wanted to speak to him. Just in time she remembered that he wasn't really there with her at all. None of them were.

There was no sound in this vision. She could hear no words. But she hoped she never saw that particular expression of unrestrained fury on Hugh's son's face. As Hugh advanced on the young Alice Todd, Corrie closed her eyes. When she opened them again, she was alone. The furniture was once more covered with drop cloths.

Suddenly weak-kneed, she sank down on the end of the bed. Why had Hugh been so angry at her mother?

"I'll check on it myself," Lucas said into the phone. A waiter had noticed there was a light on in one of the rooms in a closed wing of the hotel.

He expected to find a couple of teenagers. It wasn't unheard of for local kids, looking for a quiet and private place to make out, to sneak into an empty room at the Sinclair House. He'd done it himself once or twice when he was in high school. The doors to the rooms were kept locked, but the lack of a key had never been any match for overactive hormones.

It did surprise him that they'd left a light on. He spotted a pale yellow glow beneath a door as soon as he entered the empty wing. Grim-faced, he stalked toward it. At least they'd saved him the trouble of guessing which room they'd chosen.

The door opened easily, and Lucas stepped inside. Whatever he'd expected to find, it was not Corrie Ballantyne huddled on the edge of the bed, shivering uncontrollably. One glance at her face told him that something extraordinary had happened to her. He approached cautiously, his footfalls barely audible on the thick carpet, and called her name.

She looked up at him, a haunted expression on her pale face. "I saw her again."

"Adrienne?"

"Yes." Her bleak gaze warned him he wasn't going to like what she had to tell him. "Adrienne led me here, and I saw my mother and your father. He was yelling at her. I'm guessing she'd just told him about her sighting."

"My father does have a temper," Lucas admitted. "Exactly what did you see this time, Corrie?"

Color rushed into her face at his skeptical tone, but she complied with his request, filling in every detail she could dredge up.

As he listened, he sensed Corrie's discomfort and realized she didn't want to tell him what had happened. She was doing so only because she needed so badly to convince him it was true.

After she'd related all she'd seen, she took a deep breath. "I'd like to talk to your father."

He didn't reply, just held out his hand. She took it, following him into the hall and watching in strained silence as he locked the door behind them.

A futile gesture. Too little. Too late.

And as much as he hated to admit it, Corrie was probably right. They should talk to his father and ask him exactly what young Alice had claimed to have seen.

Thinking like that meant he was starting to believe Corrie's incredible story. The realization shook Lucas. What had happened to his common sense? His grip on reality?

They left the closed wing and reentered the warmth of the connecting corridor. "I know your father isn't able to talk," Corrie said, "but there must be some way to communicate with him."

"We've been experimenting with using a laptop computer, but even striking a key takes tremendous effort. I don't want him trying to do too much. And I don't want him getting upset."

They'd reached her room. She turned to face him, her back against the door. Obviously he wasn't going to be invited in.

"I'm not trying to cause problems, Lucas. You have to believe that. But I need to talk to him."

He did believe her. And he could tell that Corrie was not unscathed by this. She hadn't asked to be haunted. His concern for her was very nearly equal to his worry over what effect badgering his father might have on the older man's health.

"We'll talk to Pop together," he said. Questioning his own sanity would have to wait. He had enough else to worry about right now.

Her answering smile was a trifle crooked and tremendously endearing. "Thank you."

"I'll let you know when we can see him. I want to talk to his doctor first."

As he opened the door for her, his voice gentled and the sudden husky undertone had little connection to the words he actually spoke. "Just do me a favor," he said, "and stay put for the rest of the night."

At midmorning the next day, Lucas escorted Corrie to his parents' house. Hugh was waiting for them in the study, his laptop already in place on his knees, but Lucas had not yet told him the purpose of this visit.

"Pop," he began, "there have been some strange things going on at the hotel. We need your help."

There was a flicker of response in the older man's eyes. That seemed a good sign, but as Lucas pulled the desk chair close to Hugh's wheelchair and sat, he wondered just how much he really wanted to know. He was still fighting the idea that there were such things as ghosts.

"I've seen Adrienne again," Corrie said. She knelt on the other side of Hugh, so that they were eye to eye. "I'm trying to figure out what she wants, Mr. Sinclair, and to do that I need to know more about the other person who saw her. The teenage girl. She was my mother."

The look in Hugh's eyes might have been either embarrassment or guilt.

"You didn't want to believe her, did you?" Corrie asked.

Hugh made no attempt to answer.

Concerned, Lucas looked from his father to Corrie. How far did she want to pursue this? Pop already seemed uneasy, and the doctor had warned them that another stroke was possible. He'd advised keeping Hugh calm.

"Let me tell you what I've seen," Corrie said.

"I don't want you getting him stirred up," Lucas warned her.

"Lucas, he knows something about this already. He's got to be wondering what's going on. This can only help." She turned back to Hugh. "Why were they staying here?" she asked. "The hotel was closed, wasn't it?"

Hugh nodded, but he made no move to touch the keyboard. He either could not or did not want to explain.

"Did they leave because of the fire danger?"

He nodded again.

"Had they planned to come back?"

A slight negative shake answered this time.

"Do you know what Adrienne tried to tell my mother?"

Another no.

"Why were you yelling at her? I saw that much.

Adrienne showed me. You were in their room and furious at my mother. What had she said to you?"

Sweat stood out in beads on Hugh's forehead. He closed his eyes. His fingers remained motionless, as if he didn't know what he was supposed to do with the laptop.

"Corrie, that's enough!"

"But, Lucas, I—"

Her persistence goaded him into losing his temper. Seizing her by the arm, he rushed her out of the room before she could ask anything else. In the hallway, he pinned her against the wall, his hands on her shoulders, and glared down at her.

"This is my father, Corrie. Not yours. Cut him some slack."

"Lucas, this is important."

He snapped at her. "When it comes down to a choice between my family and anyone else, I put my family first."

"Anyone? Even—?"

"Even you, Corrie. The family comes before *any* woman. You want proof? My wife tried to make me choose between funneling money into the hotel we owned together and helping Pop after Kelvin's embezzlement. I'm here, aren't I? And she's not."

He raked one hand through his hair and wondered why on earth he'd mentioned Dina again. This situation was completely different. Wasn't it?

"Dammit, Lucas. What does your ex-wife have to do with Adrienne?"

"I'd have been back months earlier if I'd known the

true state of affairs at the Sinclair House. She kept that from me. Hell, I might even have been in time to prevent some of the damage Kelvin did to the hotel."

Yet even knowing what Dina had done, he remembered that the decision to leave her had not been an easy one. When he married her he'd expected they'd be together forever. He'd believed in happily ever after, thought he'd made her part of his family.

He'd been wrong.

"I'm not even going to attempt to translate that," Corrie muttered. "And for your information, I wasn't about to suggest you put me ahead of your family in the first place. It was *Adrienne* I was going to name. In case you've forgotten, she *is* family."

He felt lower than a drained pond, but it was too late to take back what he'd said. An apology seemed futile too.

"Not even for Adrienne," he told her. "I won't let Pop's health be jeopardized by more questions. Forget about finding out what happened back in 1947 and forget about whatever it is Adrienne wants you to do for her. This is all nonsense, anyway. I shouldn't have let myself be suckered into going along with it."

"It isn't nonsense, and I can't back out now."

"Corrie, there are no such things as ghosts."

Sparks seemed to fly out of her eyes. Blue fire. "You have a right to your opinion, but so do I!"

"All I ask is that you leave my father alone. If you must keep looking for answers, find them somewhere else."

"Fine!" Grabbing her coat off the hall tree as she passed it, Corrie slammed out of the house.

Lucas watched her go in growing despair, uncomfortably aware that, once again, he'd put his father's welfare before his feelings for a woman.

This time it hurt more.

He suspected memories of this particular woman would haunt him far longer than his regrets over the end of his marriage had.

Lucas called himself every kind of a fool. He wasn't married to Corrie Ballantyne. He hadn't even slept with her. What did it matter if he never saw her again? Indeed, life would be much more peaceful if she'd just leave the Sinclair House and never come back.

Refusing to acknowledge the ache that thought provoked deep in his heart, he returned to the study, where Hugh was waiting for him. The older man's eyes were alert and filled with concern.

"Is she right, Pop? Do you know something?"

Hugh struck the *N* on the computer keyboard. No.

"Would you speculate about it if you could talk to me?"

Hugh struck the *Y*.

Shaking his head, unable to think of the right questions to ask, Lucas was about to abandon this frustrating, nearly one-sided conversation when Hugh began typing one letter after another, until a question that had nothing at all to do with ghosts appeared on the laptop's small screen.

Do you love her?

"Damned if I know, Pop." Lucas tried to smile at

his father and failed. "I shouldn't. She's been nothing but trouble since she got here."

Hugh waited, this time conveying the same question with his eyes.

"I could love her," Lucas finally admitted, "if I let myself. But somehow I don't think falling in love with Corrie Ballantyne would be a very smart thing to do."

Corrie was in a bad mood when she got back to her room. Rachel had already left to go skiing. The minivan that took downhill skiers to the nearest mountain made several runs each day, but Corrie saw no point in trying to track down her friend.

Her gaze fell on the bed, and she frowned. The maid had been in. So had someone else. A small, plain brown paper bag had been left on the pillow. Cautiously, Corrie picked it up and peeked inside.

She crushed it closed again at once. Rachel. Up to her old tricks.

But on second thought, the gesture made Corrie smile. She opened the bag and stared at the wisps of black lace it contained. Extracting them with exaggerated care, she examined each of the three pieces of what could only be described as a naughty nightie.

She'd seen the outfit before, in a display at the little boutique she and Rachel had shopped in, the boutique where she'd bought the dress she was planning to wear that night for New Year's Eve.

Trust Rachel, Corrie thought wryly, to decide that lives could be improved by exchanging sensible flannel for lace. Corrie had never been much interested in fancy nightwear. Her taste ran to the practical and warm. But now that she had been given this bit of nothing, she couldn't resist the temptation to try it on.

Hastily slipping out of her clothes, she eased into a tiny triangle that was held across the hips by narrow bands of elastic. The lacy top was gathered at the waist so that it flared over her hips in a tiny skirt. It all but bared her breasts. The third piece, so transparent, it hardly qualified as a robe, hid little more.

Color crept into her cheeks as Corrie studied herself in the mirror. The peignoir was outrageously sexy, hinting at more than it actually revealed. And, impossible as it seemed to her, it made her feel . . . excited.

Would a man find it arousing? Would Lucas?

For a moment she let herself imagine his gaze moving slowly over her body, heating steadily. Yes, he'd respond to it, to her. And she wouldn't be wearing it long.

On a low moan, Corrie's lips parted. The woman in the mirror was a stranger, capable of—

Startled by the wanton direction of her thoughts, she pivoted. Her gaze fell on the bed, and her blush deepened to crimson.

Tonight was New Year's Eve. Did Lucas still want her to spend the evening with him? The night? She was no longer sure.

A week. She'd known him only a week and her life was in turmoil. She was scheduled to stay only three more nights at the Sinclair House. She wasn't sure she wanted to contemplate what could happen in that length of time.

Even scarier was the temptation to extend her vacation. She wanted to help Adrienne. She also wanted more time with Lucas. She knew already that she'd regret it for the rest of her life if she didn't see things through to some sort of conclusion.

The man had gotten under her skin. It wasn't just lust, either. She liked him . . . most of the time.

She wanted to spend the night in his arms.

Where had that thought come from?

She had to wonder. Had it been her own idea? Or had Adrienne put the notion into her head, the way she'd engineered that kiss in the sleigh? In sudden confusion, Corrie stripped off the sensually soft pieces and stuffed them back into their plain brown wrapper.

When she was safely bundled into her comfortable, all-concealing terry-cloth bathrobe, she faced the mirror again. The same old reliable, practical Corrie Ballantyne looked back at her . . . except that there was a haunted look in her eyes.

NINE

A lounge called the Tavern was located at the basement level of the Sinclair House. It had been turned into the local version of a trendy nightspot for New Year's Eve, with a singer and backup group performing and the center of the room cleared for dancing.

Before their quarrel over questioning his father, Corrie had agreed to meet Lucas there at eight. She needed only a moment to pick him out of the crowd. It wasn't that he was taller or dressed differently, though he did look magnificent in a tuxedo. Some strange, invisible current began to flow the moment they were in the same room together. She felt his presence as soon as she came through the door.

He spotted her at the same instant and smiled in her direction. She hoped that meant he'd been watching for her, anticipating her arrival. Her spirits lifted as her uncertainty faded. Whatever had passed between them earlier, he seemed glad to see her now.

With long, determined strides, he crossed the room, delayed only twice by the milling crowd. Then he was at her side. "My dance, I believe."

When he took her in his arms, Corrie knew not only that he forgave her for upsetting Hugh, but also that he approved of the cream-colored cocktail dress she wore. With a warmth that exceeded what he needed to play the suave hotelier, he pulled her closer, moving in time to the music, leading her through intricate steps with practiced skill.

Corrie rested her head against his shoulder and gave herself over to the rhythm. He was a wonderful dancer, and the way he looked at her made her feel more beautiful, more desirable, than she ever had before. She relished the blissful sensation, even though it frightened her a little.

As the old song said, it was almost like being in love.

The Tavern was crowded, with a noise level that made conversation difficult. After a time, in spite of the smoke filters in the ceiling, both Corrie and Lucas were blinking and sniffling from the presence of several cigarette smokers. As soon as the song ended, Lucas gestured toward the door.

"Air," he mouthed.

Corrie coughed delicately and nodded.

"Sorry about the cigarettes," he said as they used the back stairs to reach the second-floor ballroom, where another well-attended party was in progress.

"The smoke was bothering you too," she pointed out. "Why don't you ban them entirely?"

"I wish I could, but it would be a bad business decision. Smokers have rights. Or so they tell me. The best compromise so far is to keep all but one of the lounges smoke-free."

He swirled her into his arms again as they entered the ballroom. The group at this party was older and a bit more staid, but the waltz suited Corrie's mood. She remembered her first impression of Lucas as some sort of misanthropic English nobleman with dark secrets and smiled to herself. Tonight the image of a Regency rake seemed equally appropriate.

Curious, she turned her face toward his neck and sniffed.

"What?" he murmured.

"No bay rum," she whispered back. His start of surprise made her chuckle.

"If I'd realized you were so fond of it—"

"Just an observation, not a preference," she assured him. In fact, the woodsy scent he had on was perfect for him.

He was a man full of contradictions, she thought, equally at home at a formal affair and in a cabin surrounded by snow and trees.

The waltz ended far too soon, but Corrie let him go with good grace. She knew he had duties to perform as host. It pleased her that he chose to remain by her side as much as he could, and she tried not to resent those duty dances he bestowed on other women.

They wouldn't be with him after the dance, she told herself.

Then she stopped and wondered. Would she? Lucas hadn't said a word about how their evening was to end.

She didn't have much time to worry. Other men danced with her while Lucas circulated, and he came back to her time and time again. Swirling in his arms, she relaxed, letting herself enjoy the evening.

At ten minutes before midnight, he spirited her away from the crowd, giving her only time enough to collect her evening bag while he stopped for two glasses of champagne. Once more they used the narrow back stairs, but this time their destination was the Fireside Room. Lucas closed the door behind them to ensure privacy.

After the noise and crowding in the Tavern and the more subtle gaiety of the ballroom, it was almost too quiet in the deeply carpeted room. A fire burned fitfully in the hearth, providing the only illumination other than the Christmas tree, which had been lit for one last night, and a single table lamp. Lucas handed Corrie both glasses and switched off the light, leaving them in romantic, multicolored shadows, before he went to stir the embers.

"Back where it all began," she murmured as she watched the fabric shift and tighten over the backs of his thighs when he bent, then straightened again.

She didn't think Lucas heard her, but he had to be thinking the same thing. Only a week ago, she'd stood there and watched him. And he'd watched her.

Returning to her side, he took one glass and

toasted her with the champagne. "To a new year," he said. "To new beginnings."

She clinked her glass lightly against his, wondering what exactly he had in mind. If the smoldering look in his eyes was anything to go by, he had very specific plans for the two of them.

Suddenly nervous, she was awkward when he slipped his arm through hers so they could sip from each other's glasses, but at least they managed not to spill any.

"Hard to believe we met just a week ago in this very room," he said, echoing her earlier thoughts.

"A lot has certainly happened since then."

She was thinking about the two of them, but she made the mistake of glancing over his shoulder . . . directly at Adrienne's portrait. She jerked her gaze away, remembering the resolution she'd made earlier in the evening. She'd promised herself she would not dwell on anything unpleasant that night and for some reason Adrienne seemed to fall into that category.

"I was a fool to try to resist you," Lucas said.

"Christmas Eve was a wonderful night all the same," she assured him, "and I thought you sang beautifully."

He chuckled and took that as a hint. Catching her hand, he drew her after him to the piano. "Sit," he ordered, tugging until she was beside him on the bench. Then he set aside his champagne glass and picked out the first notes of "Some Enchanted Evening."

"Sing with me," he invited.

"I wish I could. My voice is hopeless."

"It sounds sweet to my ears."

She smacked him on the arm. "Don't overdo the flattery, Sinclair. I'll think you're just playing perfect host again."

In the firelight, she saw his face go abruptly serious. "All right," he agreed. "No games, Corrie. No humoring you. And no preconceived notions about where we're headed. I don't have any idea, but it doesn't seem to matter at the moment."

Her glass joined his on the end table next to the piano. In the distance she could hear the whistles and shouts of revelers as the new year arrived, but Corrie's focus was entirely fixed on Lucas Sinclair as he gathered her into his arms. He held her as carefully as if she were a statue made of spun glass.

"Happy New Year, Corrie."

"Happy New Year, Lucas."

His kiss started out gentle and heated slowly. Corrie responded to it with every fiber of her being, flowing against him as her arms crept around his neck, her fingers tunneling into his thick dark hair.

With the gentlest of touches of his mouth, he urged her lips apart, sipping at her with a quiet intensity more demanding than a rough kiss. She let her eyes drift closed, the better to savor both his response and her own.

For endless moments they clung together, absorbing from each other the essence of tender caring. It seemed to Corrie she'd been waiting her whole life to be held this way.

Before long, she was unable to resist looking at him again. She opened her eyes to the sight of pure passion in the mobile features of his face. She felt her own eyelashes flutter as she realized he was watching her every bit as intently, looking for some sign from her. When he recognized it, his eyes darkened to deepest amber. His pupils grew huge with arousal. A shiver of desire shuddered through Corrie at the sight.

The yearning, the longing, was mutual.

Her fingers stroked again through his softly waving hair. His hands dropped to her waist, then slid lower, tugging her tight against him on the narrow piano bench.

Lost in the sensuality of the moment, Corrie clung to him, her senses reeling. Her eyes were still open as his lips moved along her jawline and dipped down to the exposed flesh of her neck.

And then, over his shoulder, she noticed the portrait again. Stiffening, she tried to pull away. "It's too public here," she whispered.

His head snapped up, a dazed look on his face. After a moment he managed a weak smile. "You make me forget everything but you."

"I'm flattered," she said, teasing him. "For a minute there, I don't believe you even knew we were still at the hotel."

His expression was rueful, his voice gruff. "You're right. You have a powerful effect on me, Corrie Ballantyne."

Then he sighed. "I have one or two things to see to before I'm through for the night."

"I understand." But she knew her disappointment must be evident in her voice.

"May I come to your room later, when I'm free?"

Still held close to him, breathing his fresh scent, one hand touching the silky softness of his hair and the other resting against the fine fabric of his shirt, Corrie kept her eyes away from the fireplace, but she didn't have to see Adrienne's portrait to be reminded of the terrible truth. There was nowhere in this hotel where she wouldn't feel a ghostly presence.

The idea of an invisible witness to all they did was not conducive to making love with Lucas.

"I'm not sure coming to my room is such a good idea," she murmured.

Very carefully, he set her away from him. An acute awkwardness settled between them, almost palpable in the quiet, dimly lit room.

Lucas hesitated, then said, "We can just go back to the party if you like."

"That's not exactly what I meant," she whispered.

Being with Lucas had definite appeal, but only if she felt she could trust her own judgment. As far as she had been able to observe, Adrienne only knew, and could only show Corrie, and could only control things that happened in the hotel or within sight of its windows. If they were somewhere else, then anything that happened between herself and Lucas would be because *Corrie* wanted it.

She was appalled by the brazenness of what she meant to suggest, but she could not face the thought of ending her relationship with Lucas without ever knowing the sweetness of making love with him.

This was crazy. She knew that. Their timing couldn't have been worse. But there was something good between them, something that deserved a chance to grow.

Her vacation was almost over, she reminded herself. It would be better not to start anything.

But it was already started.

And it didn't have to end just because there was going to be some geographical distance between them. She was enough of a realist to know that long-distance romances rarely worked, but this was Lucas. She had to try.

"Could we go to your cabin instead?" she asked.

Everything he wanted was his for the taking, but Lucas paused to enjoy a slow, appreciative perusal of the woman he held in his arms. They were in his bed, flesh to flesh, but this was about more than sex. He'd never felt such a sense of rightness in these moments prior to making love.

"Elegant," he murmured.

She started to protest.

With just his fingertips he traced the curve of her eyebrows. His other hand caressed her silken shoulder.

"You have no idea, have you, of how perfect you are?"

Rather than let her reply, he sealed her lips with a kiss of devastating thoroughness. They were both breathless when they came up for air . . . and pressed as close together as two people could be without actually being joined.

"You seem pretty perfect to me, too, just now." Her eyes dark with passion, she gazed up at him.

There was a rightness about the two of them, he thought. Here. Together. Lucas made no attempt to analyze the feeling. He simply accepted it. This was meant to be. He and Corrie were destined to find each other, to revel in their mutual discovery of joy. Of love.

From that point on, he made love to her in reverent silence, letting his body speak for him. With infinite slowness, prolonging the pleasure, he touched and stroked, delved and sipped.

Corrie answered his tender caresses with her own, exploring him as he learned her secrets. Together they built toward the moment when need overcame control. He barely had the presence of mind to fumble for protection before they were swept as one into a soul-shattering, mind-bending race to completion.

It was magnificent.

And it was over far too soon.

Utter contentment filled Corrie's heart as she woke with her head nestled against Lucas's chest. She was still savoring the afterglow of the most memorable lovemaking she'd ever experienced.

Momentarily sated, she had no interest in Monday-morning quarterbacking. They'd taken this step in their relationship with their eyes open, and it had been the right thing to do. She had no idea what would happen next, and at that precise moment, she couldn't find energy enough to care.

She could, however, find sufficient strength to respond when Lucas awoke and kissed the healing gash on her forehead.

Such a little thing, an act of caring, of kindness, yet it triggered so much more. They were lying too close together for her to miss his reaction.

Just as quickly, she wanted him again too.

A giggle escaped her. "Insatiable," she whispered. "Am I alone in that?"

"Not a chance."

This time she took the lead, showing him just how much she shared his desire, his need. Touching him was pure pleasure. Easing herself slowly along his body until she straddled him, kissing every available surface in her path, she brought them together in a fiery consummation every bit as satisfying as their first encounter.

One arm lay on the pillow, extended so that she could see her watch without moving. It was past noon. Corrie lay perfectly still for several minutes more, reconstructing the events of the early-morning hours. She could hear Lucas moving about in the kitchen below.

Smiling, she sat up and made a quick survey of her surroundings. Her overnight bag was on the floor by a chair. She'd never had a chance to open it and take out her nightwear, let alone hang up a change of clothes. Her things would be hopelessly rumpled, but she didn't imagine Lucas would care.

After a quick shower, she put on jeans and a turtleneck, made the bed, and swept the curtains aside to reveal a bright, sun-dappled day. The bedroom windows took up nearly the entire wall, floor to roof beams, and gave her a splendid view.

Lucas had heard the shower and had a cup of coffee ready for her when she came down. She accepted it gratefully.

"Thank you." She sipped at the hot beverage, inhaling the fragrant steam. Everything seemed more sensuous this morning, more vivid.

"So," he asked, "what shall we do today? I don't have to be back to work until tomorrow morning."

She grinned at him. "It's New Year's Day, isn't it? What else would we do but watch bowl games?"

"You like football?"

His astonishment amused her, but also made her aware of how little they really knew about each other. "As it happens," she informed him, "I'm a rabid football fan, especially when my old college team is playing."

For the rest of the afternoon and into the evening, they got to know each other in many little ways, happily munching popcorn and watching football games while they engaged in quiet conversation. They covered most of the subjects normal couples discussed, and with each passing hour Corrie felt more at ease with Lucas.

They did not talk about family.

They did not mention ghosts.

Old acquaintances by then, they moved on to cook dinner together and share the dishwashing duties. After that, when Lucas went to get wood for the fireplace, Corrie curled up with her feet beneath her on his sofa, leaving room for him to join her there. She couldn't remember when she'd felt more comfortable with anyone.

After Lucas had a cheerful blaze going, he took the seat, snaking one arm around her waist and pulling her tight against his side. From behind his back he drew out a gift for her, a perfectly shaped pinecone.

"I'll treasure it always," she promised. Then she frowned, remembering a snippet of conversation from the day she and Rachel had shared brunch with Joyce. "What's a cone year? I heard your mother use the term but I never got a chance to ask her what it meant."

Lucas grinned and nuzzled her earlobe. "It has to do with the sex lives of pine trees."

"You're making that up," she said as a delicate shudder passed through her. Just that fast she wanted him again.

"Nope. White pines have male and female cones. A cone year comes once every five years or so, when all the trees have more cones than usual. That produces more pollen, which fertilizes the female cones. It also makes the trees more flammable."

"How . . . fascinating." He was now nibbling on her neck, making it hard for her to concentrate on their conversation.

"Want to play pine trees?" he asked in a wicked whisper. "You can be the female and I'll be the male."

Corrie tried to hold back a giggle but it was no use. The first burst of mirth was followed by a full-bodied laugh. Once started, she couldn't seem to stop.

After a moment, Lucas joined in, reaching for her and holding her close while they both whooped without restraint.

It was cleansing. Cathartic. And when the laughter finally subsided an even more powerful force took its place.

Renewed desire hummed between them, impossible to ignore, impossible to deny. Corrie cleared her throat, remembering what she had packed in that overnight case upstairs.

"How do you feel about black peignoirs?" she asked.

TEN

Adrienne Sinclair was upset.

She wasn't able to make contact with Corrie because Corrie was not at the Sinclair House.

That she might not be successful in conveying the information, even if Corrie were in the hotel, was not the point. It was devilishly frustrating that she did not even have the opportunity to try.

Pacing the confines of Corrie's room, Adrienne did the only thing she could—she waited. Surely Corrie would come back.

As Adrienne kicked a slipper out of her way, she realized that most of Corrie's clothes were still in the room. With renewed hope, she went through every item in the armoire. She was uncertain what she was seeking until she found a navy blue blazer. A pin in the shape of a particular flower had been fastened to the lapel.

Perfect.

Adrienne moved the small object to a more prominent

location, one guaranteed to attract Corrie's attention as soon as she returned.

"I wish I didn't have to go back to the hotel," Lucas said as he finished his second cup of morning coffee. "I wish you didn't have to."

Two nights and an entire day together hadn't been nearly enough time alone with Corrie. His cabin was going to feel lonely without her, but it was way too early in their relationship to ask her to move in with him.

Wasn't it?

"That's one nice thing about freelance work," she said. "I have a lot of choice about when and where I put in my hours." She was washing out her own cup. Her overnight bag stood packed and ready by the door.

Scarcely daring to hope, Lucas walked up behind her at the sink, so close he could shadow her arms as he dumped the dregs of his coffee down the drain. "Does that mean you could stay on longer if you wanted to?"

"If *you* wanted me to," she said softly, "then I suppose I could. For a few more days, anyway."

Aware his thoughts were growing far too serious way too fast, he retreated into humor, mimicking Rachel's accent. "I could give you such a deal—"

"I'll bet you could," she murmured, turning in his arms.

"I'll have the rest of your things packed and sent over from the hotel—" At the look on her face he broke off. "What?"

"Lucas, if I stay it should be at the Sinclair House." She squirmed in his grip. "Oh, drat! This isn't going to work."

Bewildered, he stepped back. His hands still resting lightly on her forearms, he could feel the fine trembling that shook her.

"Corrie, what is it? I thought you said there was no problem with your job?"

"There isn't. I can work anywhere, up to a point." She wouldn't meet his eyes, and she began to talk faster and faster, without revealing what was really bothering her. "My clients like to talk to me face-to-face occasionally, but most of the business is done electronically. I have my laptop computer with me. I can get quite a bit of work done in my hotel room. That would be better, really."

"If that's true, you could work here just as easily." He was beginning to have a bad feeling about this, but he did want her to stay, if not with him then at the hotel. He needed time to figure out how to keep the two of them together longer.

He knew he was rushing things, but he couldn't help thinking that if her job was that flexible, then it was possible she might move her business to Maine entirely. Or at least open a branch office there.

She sighed and finally met his eyes. "You aren't the only one who wants me to stay on, but she needs me to be at the Sinclair House, since that's the only place I've ever seen her."

"Adrienne?" Lucas felt his temper rising and clamped down on it, but not before he'd flexed his hands on Corrie's arms hard enough to make her wince. Hastily, he released her. She turned away from him and gathered up her parka.

"I haven't managed to do whatever it is she wants me to do, have I? I don't even know what it is yet."

Lucas was not at all pleased by the reminder. He supposed he'd been hoping she'd forgotten all about that damned ghost. He helped her into her coat and shrugged into his own, making one last attempt to get her to stay.

"You could sleep here, Corrie, and just visit the hotel during the day. Not that I'm agreeing it could happen, but if *you* think she might be turning up when we'd, er, rather be alone, then—"

"If I go back, I'll be available to both of you." Her cheeks were tinged with pink. "Except in that one way, of course."

"What are you suggesting, Corrie? That we be reduced to coming back here for an occasional nooner?"

She blinked at him in surprise, taken aback by the bite in his words. Maybe he'd been wrong, he thought. If she didn't understand how he felt about this supernatural crap, what real hope did they have for a future together?

"Lucas," she said gently, reaching up to touch his jaw with her fingertips. Just that slight contact jolted through him like an electric shock. "I'm sorry you're upset by my sense of obligation to Adrienne, but I am committed to going on."

He sought in vain for the words to convince her to give up her quest. He did not believe in the paranormal. She already knew that. It was a mark of how much he cared for her that he'd endured as much talk about it as he had, but now she'd stretched his patience to the limit.

If she'd been anyone else but the woman he loved, he'd have kicked her out of his hotel, out of his life, long before now.

Corrie sighed again as they stepped out into the crisp New England morning and walked toward the van. "It hurts to know something is true and have my belief tolerated rather than accepted," she said.

"I can't change my convictions any more than you can, Corrie."

"At least we're honest with each other." She sounded resigned but terribly unhappy, as if she felt this spelled the beginning of the end of their relationship.

"Corrie, don't give up on us." She was seated in the van now. He stood next to it, her hands clasped in his, looking up into her eyes.

"I have to resolve the mystery of Adrienne Sinclair if we're to have any hope of working things out between us."

Not what he wanted to hear.

He released her and stalked around to the driver's side. He could see it all now—the two of them recruited to appear on some tacky television talk show with the theme "Women Who See Ghosts and the Men Who Love Them Anyway."

They were halfway back to the hotel before he spoke again. "What do you want to do next?" he asked. "About Adrienne, I mean."

"Oh, Lucas. I wish I knew."

He was trying. He really was. But her vagueness didn't help. Why couldn't she just decide she'd imagined the whole thing and let them get on with what was really important?

Sliding toward him, she rested her head against his shoulder. "I can't seem to think what to do about anything, not even how I feel about what's happening between us."

"You don't imagine Adrienne pushed us into bed together, I hope."

That won a faint chuckle from Corrie. "No. I know for certain whose idea that was."

Remind her of how good it was, he told himself. Avoid talking about the supernatural.

But the second part of that plan couldn't work without Corrie's cooperation and she seemed determined to discuss Adrienne.

"It's the whole problem of what she wants." Corrie sat up as the hotel came into view. "That's what keeps nagging at me. I've thought over everything she's conveyed to me, and there's just no rhyme or reason to it. Most of the time I don't think I've even gotten half of what she's trying to tell me."

"Maybe there's a simple explanation for that," he

muttered as he stopped the van under the portico. He waved off the valet, needing a few more minutes of privacy.

"And that is?" Corrie's tone was brittle, as if she, too, had reached the end of her rope on this subject.

"Maybe what you've seen of Adrienne had more to do with that knock you took to the head than you're willing to admit. Maybe—"

She reached for the door handle. He barely caught her in time to keep her from opening it, grasping her groping fingers with one hand and gripping the shoulder closest to him with the other.

"It's no good, Corrie. I want you in my life. I can accept that you sincerely believe you saw Adrienne. That doesn't affect the way I feel about you. But you'll have to accept the truth sometime. She isn't real, Corrie. There are no such things as ghosts."

Corrie's eyes were downcast. He felt a shiver shudder through her slender frame. "I was wrong," she murmured.

His heart leapt with hope. "Thank God."

Finally, she looked up at him. "Not about Adrienne. About us."

Tears welled up and slid down her cheeks. Confused, he could only stare helplessly at her.

"I thought it didn't matter," she whispered. "That I could continue looking for Adrienne and you would tolerate my doing so. But this goes deeper, doesn't it? It isn't just that you don't believe in ghosts, Lucas. It's that you don't have any faith in me."

❖━━━━━❖

When Corrie returned to her hotel room, alone, she noticed the lapel pin lying on top of the Sinclair family tree. She automatically picked it up, went to the armoire, and pinned it back on the blazer where it belonged. Then she returned the chart to its file folder.

Her mind was elsewhere.

The night before at Lucas's cabin, sometime after he'd demonstrated his appreciation of black peignoirs, she'd come to a realization. She'd gone and fallen in love with the man.

It seemed impossible after knowing him such a short time, but she didn't question her conclusion. No other emotion could account for the way she felt— elated and totally miserable at the same time.

"Great timing, Corrie," she grumbled to herself. "And so intelligent too."

For in spite of their traumatic scene in the van just now, she still hoped they might have a future together. Could she plan forever with a man who couldn't believe what she said without outside proof? That did not bode well for a trusting relationship.

It did not, however, mean he didn't love her.

Her first reaction had been to think that if he loved her, he'd accept her beliefs even if he did not share them. That Lucas had tried to change her mind had been a crushing blow. But now that she'd had time to think, she realized there might have been another reason for what he was doing. If he did love her, it made sense that he might fear for her sanity in a situation he did not understand.

She wasn't happy with that explanation, but she *could* put herself in his place. After all, she hadn't wanted to believe in ghosts at first, either.

Corrie thought about going down to his office to try again to explain herself, but she fought the impulse. It was too soon. They both needed time to cool down. Barge in on him now and they'd only end up quarreling again.

There was but one chance for them. She had to fulfill Adrienne's mission. Only then would she be free to build a future with Lucas.

She was startled when a knock sounded at her bedroom door. Not Adrienne, she thought with a wry smile. That much was certain.

"Who is it?" she called out.

"It's your father." Donald Ballantyne's gruff voice was unmistakable.

"Daddy?" she whispered in astonishment.

"Corrie, let me in." He sounded worried.

She quickly opened the door, then froze. For the first time, Corrie saw how elderly her father looked. He'd aged a great deal in the last year, until he seemed almost . . . frail.

"Daddy, what are you doing here?" She managed to get that much out before she was engulfed in a bear hug. He didn't *feel* frail. Relief surged through her at that realization.

"I tried phoning you yesterday. Couldn't reach you."

Holding her away from him, he studied her, taking in the scab on her forehead and probably noticing the shadows under her eyes as well. She didn't think she wanted to explain to him the reason she hadn't gotten much sleep either of the last two nights. Or where she'd been.

"I had a nice drive up," he told her. "Started yesterday afternoon. Stayed over in Vermont. Came the rest of the way today. Rachel's been entertaining me while we waited for you to get back."

His gaze fell on her overnight bag, still packed, sitting on the floor by the bed.

How much, Corrie wondered, had Rachel told him? For all the problems between them, he was still her father, and a father tended to condemn any man he suspected of sleeping with his little girl.

That was all she needed—a duel over her honor!

But Donald Ballantyne avoided that subject entirely. Instead he held up one finger to indicate she should wait a minute and ducked back across the hall to Rachel's room.

Rachel appeared in the open doorway and gave Corrie a what-else-could-I-do shrug as her father retrieved his suitcase. Later, Rachel would no doubt want a full report on the time Corrie had spent with Lucas, as well as on the forthcoming session with her father, but at the moment she seemed relieved to be out of the line of fire.

Donald put the heavy suitcase on Corrie's bed to open it. He looked a little embarrassed. "After I couldn't reach you by phone, I realized it would be easier to show you what I found. This way you can explain to me what it all means."

He withdrew a heavy leather-bound book from the battered Samsonite case that dated from the time before soft-sided luggage. "I found that photograph you asked about. It was marking a page in this."

"This" was the family Bible, and the marked page was one on which births were entered. The first name leapt out at Corrie: Marguerite Mead, born May 5, 1878, Waycross Springs, Maine.

"I don't understand," Corrie murmured. What was Marguerite from the Mead/Sinclair family tree doing in Alice Ballantyne's family Bible?

"I noticed the town," her father said. "I figured there must be some connection."

"To *Marguerite*?"

"Your mother always called her Daisy," he explained. "Look on the page for marriages."

The name there was "Daisy Skinner, widow."

The pieces of the puzzle suddenly fell into place. Just as the second Marguerite Mead, Stanley Kelvin's mother, had used the nickname Rita, the first had gone by Daisy. Marguerite Mead Skinner Hanover was Horatio Mead's missing daughter. She was also Corrie's great-grandmother.

Corrie couldn't imagine why she hadn't seen it sooner. Oh, the fact that the Meads and Sinclairs apparently thought Marguerite had died at the age of eighteen had thrown her off, and she still couldn't explain that mistake on Joyce's chart, but she'd known ever since high school language classes that *marguerite* was French for daisy. And the pin she'd found not an hour earlier on the dresser was shaped like a daisy. Obviously Adrienne had left that, and on top of the red file folder containing the Sinclair family tree.

"Okay, Adrienne," she said softly. "I've got it now."

"Corrie?"

Her father sounded puzzled. And concerned.

"Thanks, Daddy," she said. "You have no idea how important this is." She set the Bible aside to hug him, whispering, "I'm glad you came."

He seemed pleased by her words and hugged her back. Then, both of them a little embarrassed by the display of emotion, they separated. Donald went to stand by the window and look out at the snow-covered landscape.

"Wanted to see the place for myself," he said after a moment. "For Alice's sake." He fell silent again, as if he was carefully weighing his words. When he spoke, his voice sounded gruffer. "Wanted to spend some time with my only daughter too. I don't want to lose you, Corrie. Family's pretty important. Maybe the most important thing there is in life."

"Oh, Daddy." She knew how hard it had been for him to express his feelings. In swift steps she crossed the room to stand beside him. "You're so right."

For the next half hour, they said things to each other that should have been said years earlier. Corrie was just glad they hadn't waited any longer, that they hadn't missed this chance.

"Family's important," her father said again. "That's why I had to come in person."

She laughed softly, remembering what he'd brought her. It seemed they were *all* one family here.

"What's so funny?" her father asked.

She told him some of what had been happening to her at the Sinclair House. He didn't even blink at the idea of his daughter seeing a ghost.

"And if there weren't already clues enough to show that our Daisy and Horatio's Marguerite were the same person," she concluded, "then there's the name of Marguerite's mother on Joyce's chart. She was Cordelia La Fleur. I imagine I was named after her."

"Could well be that you were. I remember your mother saying she'd gotten the name from somewhere way back in your grandmother's family."

"So now all I have to do is figure out what Adrienne wants me to do with this information. At least now that I know I'm descended from her niece, I can understand why she was able to communicate with me. And with Mama. I just wish I knew what it was that turned Adrienne into a ghost in the first place and how I'm supposed to help her find peace."

"You'll figure it out and then you'll find a way," her father said. "You're resourceful. Always have been. Your mother was very proud of you and so am I."

"Thanks, Daddy. I wish everyone had that much faith in me."

"Everyone? Or just this Lucas Sinclair?"

In her account of the events since Christmas Eve, Corrie had tried to gloss over her feelings for Lucas, since their future was so uncertain. She'd avoided mentioning New Year's Eve and the following day and night entirely. Her father hadn't been fooled, though. She suspected he'd gotten an earful from Rachel, and his paternal instinct was strong as well.

"Corrie," he asked, "are you in love with this man?"

When she didn't answer, he patted her hand.

"Never mind. I'll take a look at the fellow for myself. Did I tell you I promised to buy Rachel lunch?" He headed for the door. "Join us?"

What choice did she have? It was nearly lunchtime and she had to eat. Besides, with any luck at all, if they ate in the hotel dining room, she'd get another chance to communicate with Adrienne.

They collected Rachel and went down to the lobby. Lucas caught sight of them as they exited the elevator. For an instant, as he stared at her father's hand on her arm, Corrie saw a flash of what was unmistakably jealousy in his eyes.

She found that reassuring.

Introductions were stilted, but passed without incident, though Rachel was chortling to herself as they entered the dining room.

Conversation turned general over lunch. Corrie had just begun to relax when her father dropped the next bombshell.

"I think I'll stay a few days here at the Sinclair House," he announced.

Corrie bit back a groan. She was glad of the chance

to finish mending fences with her father, but she shuddered to think of the effect his presence might have on her unsettled relationship with Lucas.

She also had the uneasy feeling they'd just acquired one more matchmaker.

ELEVEN

Corrie expected some sign from Adrienne.

After her father left her in her room on his way to take Joyce up on her invitation, made as they were leaving the dining room, to introduce him to Lucas's father, Corrie stood still and waited.

Nothing happened.

She frowned, realizing she hadn't actually seen Adrienne since the ghost led her to that room in the closed portion of the hotel. But surely it had been Adrienne who'd taken the daisy pin off her lapel and left it out where Corrie would see it. Why hadn't she materialized again?

Pacing in her room, Corrie tried to put together all she knew. What Adrienne had said about Jonathan came back to her. What if he was literally a bastard? Then Marguerite would have been the legitimate Mead heir.

That meant the Phoenix Inn should have descended to Corrie and her brothers instead of to Stanley Kelvin.

There were too many cloudy areas, where she had only guesswork to guide her. It was obvious Marguerite had not died at eighteen. It looked as if she'd run away from home instead, and somehow ended up in New York State. She'd probably eloped. With Mr. Skinner, whoever he had been.

But why had anyone thought Marguerite was dead?

Adrienne must have known where her niece was. Had she meant to tell Horatio and died before she could? Or was there more to it? More to do with Jonathan?

Even if she never learned the remaining details, at least one thing made sense to Corrie. Her psychic link with Adrienne was the result of a blood relationship. Through her mother, Corrie, like Adrienne, was a descendant of Micah Mead.

Was that what Adrienne had been trying to get across to her all this time? Had Adrienne been condemned to haunt the hotel until she could reveal the truth about Jonathan and Marguerite?

But what *was* the truth? This was mostly supposition on Corrie's part. The possibility that she might never have an explanation for being haunted bothered her a great deal.

On impulse, she positioned herself on the bed, flat on her back, and stared up at the high ceiling. In the past, Adrienne had been able to influence her dreams. Maybe that was the key. Deliberately, she emptied her mind of everything except an image of the Sinclair House's resident ghost.

Focus, she told herself. Be open to anything.

She felt very heavy at first, and then as if she were floating.

She slept.

"*Horatio will not thank you for interfering,*" *a male voice said.* "*He may not even let you through the door of the Phoenix Inn. It's been six years since you married me against his wishes and he hasn't spoken to either of us since.*"

"*I know that.*" *Adrienne hated the feud, but there seemed no way to end it, especially not now.*

"*Miss Cordelia La Fleur may just make him a very good wife,*" *Lucas said.*

"*She's an actress.*"

Lucas chuckled. "*You say that in the same tone of voice you'd use to say she was a whore. They aren't the same thing, you know.*"

Adrienne tried another tack. "*Would the child's real father wed her if he were free to?*"

"*The point is moot. He can't marry her and that's enough said. Let it be, Adrienne.*"

"*The child will be a bastard.*"

"*You can still regard it as your niece or nephew. I do not see why this should bother you so much. Your brother made his own bed. Now let him lie in it. You owe him nothing.*"

"*That's right. Blame it all on my brother. You Sinclairs have been just as bad as any Mead when it comes to this* rivalry between the two families. You talk as though you think Horatio deserves to be deceived."

Lucas didn't trouble to deny it. "It will make matters worse if you interfere at this juncture. The wedding is tomorrow. If nothing else, then think of that child. What will happen to it, and to Cordelia, if Horatio doesn't marry her? How will she care for a baby alone? And don't say we can help, because to do so would only create more scandal."

"I do not like keeping secrets."

"It will be all right." Lucas nuzzled her ear. She inhaled the scent of bay rum. "Trust me, Adrienne. I know what is best to do."

Distracted by his kisses, by the desire he sparked in her so effortlessly, Adrienne said no more, but she was not easy in her mind.

Corrie stirred restlessly in the old-fashioned bed as vestiges of long-ago passion tickled her subconscious.

Both Lucas Sinclairs were marvelous lovers.

Both were stubborn and opinionated and sure their view was the only right way to look at things.

The dream faded, but in a little while it was replaced by another.

This time Adrienne lay in the bed in the room that was now Corrie's. She was alone, obviously older, and plainly in ill health. Coughs racked her. She was running a high fever. And she missed Lucas horribly.

He'd gone to Boston on business the very day the influenza struck. Nearly all the hotel staff were sick with it. By the time he returned in another week, some would have *recovered and others would most likely be dead. In the last epidemic, four Waycross Springs citizens had expired.*

The young man came in without knocking and stood near the footboard, glaring down at Adrienne with ill-concealed dislike. "I intercepted your letter to my father," he said. "He will not be coming here to listen to your ranting. There is no reason he need ever know the truth."

"You lied to him." Adrienne had to whisper her hoarse accusation. "You told him Marguerite was dead." Another bout of coughing left her struggling for breath.

"The slut eloped. Left the family. She's as good as dead to us now."

Adrienne tried to gather the strength to argue with him, but she grew weaker by the minute. She was dying. She knew that now. Dying without ever having told Horatio the truth.

"What's the matter, old woman?" Jonathan taunted her.

Bastard, she thought, but she could not give voice to the word. The room was growing dark. There was no more light, no more air.

Jonathan's triumphant laughter was the last thing she heard.

Corrie woke in a cold sweat.
Wow!
That had been more than she bargained for.
She couldn't stop shaking.
Swinging her trembling legs over the side of the bed, she tried to stand and ended up falling back onto

the mattress. Slowly her breathing steadied and her mind began to work again.

Now what?

She'd had her theories confirmed, but what would be the point of revealing what she knew? To discredit Jonathan? Why bother after all this time? The only person who would be hurt was Stanley Kelvin. It didn't seem right that the sins of the great-grandfather should be visited upon the great-grandson.

What did Adrienne want her to do?

Tell the true story, obviously. It seemed important to the ghost that people know Marguerite had survived and was the legitimate heiress of the Meads.

But challenging inheritance rights at this late date seemed awfully petty. She supposed such things had been considered more important in the old days, but it didn't make much difference to her who owned the Phoenix Inn. She certainly didn't want it.

Perhaps Adrienne, confined as she was to the Sinclair House, didn't know the Phoenix Inn was in disrepair, that the Mead inheritance had dwindled to almost nothing.

Revealing the truth to the remaining members of each family would have to be enough for Adrienne, Corrie decided. She would tell the Sinclairs what she'd deduced. But first she must inform Stanley Kelvin.

Before she could change her mind, she reached for the phone and put through a call to the Phoenix Inn. She introduced herself to Kelvin, then said, "I'd like to discuss the feud between your family and the Sinclairs."

To her surprise, he didn't ask why. "Be at the Phoenix in an hour," he told her, then abruptly broke the connection.

Corrie wondered if she was making a mistake. Still, it seemed only fair to tell Kelvin what she'd figured out about Jonathan and Marguerite. She'd assure him that she had no intention of making the information public and then leave. Once all the Mead and Sinclair descendants knew the truth, Adrienne would be free.

Filled with a new sense of purpose, Corrie headed for Lucas's office. Before she left, she'd have just enough time to bring him up to date.

One look at Corrie made Lucas realize how impossible it would be to let her go without a fight. He simply could not imagine a future without her in it.

Standing in a sunbeam, she hesitated in his doorway. She brought light into the room with her. Literally and figuratively.

He wanted to wake up each day looking into that perfectly sculpted face, those gloriously blue eyes, touching those feather-soft tresses.

Her delicate perfume wafted across the office toward him, as light and free-spirited as she was.

Then he noticed the wariness in her stance. And the fact that she was carrying her coat. Was she going somewhere for a few hours? Or leaving for good?

His heart in his throat, he looked for luggage in the lobby behind her before she closed the door. He saw none, but he was not entirely reassured.

Hiding his joy and his torment at seeing her again before he'd decided how to handle the tricky situation between them, he asked after her father.

"You're stuck with both of us for a few days longer," she said.

"Good."

"Maybe."

She'd managed a faint smile, but the expression faded as she hesitated just inside the door. For a moment he thought she might turn around and leave again without speaking, but then she crossed the office and seated herself in the chair that faced him. Lucas fought the urge to go down on his knees in front of her and beg her forgiveness for doubting anything she'd ever told him.

While he was there he could ask her to marry him.

Unfortunately, he had to be honest. He still didn't believe in ghosts. Which brought him around to the problem of a future with Corrie. Was it impossible? Could he spend the rest of his life with a woman who was convinced she'd had supernatural experiences?

"Any sign of Adrienne since you've been back?" he asked. Might as well get it out in the open.

"Yes, as a matter of fact."

In succinct sentences, she told him what the Hanover family Bible had contained, then recounted the events she'd watched unfold in her subsequent dreams. Her conclusions were logical enough . . . if one believed in the paranormal.

"You can't deny the birth and marriage entries in the Bible," she said.

"You're right." Food for thought there. "That means you're *already* family," he murmured.

"Already?"

"Never mind that now. What you say makes sense. Some sense, anyway." She'd thrown a lot at him.

It was a helluva coincidence that she'd come to Waycross Springs, where her ancestor had lived. Still, it might be accounted for by some childhood memory of her mother talking about a similar visit.

But a ghost?

He didn't think so.

Corrie faced him from the other side of the desk, defiance in the set of her shoulders. "I've arranged to meet Stanley Kelvin in a little while. I mean to tell him what I've learned of the family history."

He shot out of his chair, barely able to stop himself from shouting at her. "What the hell do you want to go and do that for?"

"Because that's what Adrienne wants of me, Lucas. I have to tell him the same things I've just told you."

"There's no need to talk to Kelvin. Let him go on believing he owns the Phoenix." He strode around the desk and tugged her to her feet. This was a *bad* idea, but how could he convince Corrie of that?

She glanced at her watch. "I'm going to be late if I don't go now. I'll be back before you know it, Lucas, and then it will all be over. Adrienne will be gone."

"Don't go."

"I have to."

"Dammit, Corrie." He couldn't seem to find the words to explain. With no other resort left, he gathered her close and kissed her, putting everything he felt for her into that one desperate act.

She responded instantly, sweetly, but after a moment she began to ease out of the embrace.

"I love you, Corrie."

"I love you, too, but I have to do this."

"I don't want you near him. He's dangerous, Corrie. Unstable. And if you tell him the Sinclair House has a ghost, he'll—"

"What touching faith you have in me. I've no intention of saying anything about Adrienne. I'll let him think I found all this information in family records."

"Oh, that will really go over well. Make him think you have documented proof that he could lose the only thing he seems to care about."

"I'll reassure him. After all, I don't want his hotel." She broke free and slipped into her parka, bullheaded as ever. "Don't worry, Lucas. It'll be fine. You'll see. I'll come straight here as soon as I get back."

"Corrie, I know what I'm talking about. Kelvin hates anything to do with the Sinclairs. He won't react well to what you have to say and if he's heard gossip that you're involved with me, that will make him even more unpredictable." Kelvin could well know all about their relationship. Waycross Springs was a very small town.

She'd reached the door.

"Dammit, Corrie. Why can't you trust me on this?"

"Because you aren't rational where Stanley Kelvin is concerned. Besides, no woman with any sense should take for granted that a man knows what's best. If Adrienne hadn't listened to her Lucas, if she'd gone and talked to her brother as she wanted to, none of this would have been necessary."

On that note, she sailed out of his office, closing the door firmly behind her.

Lucas slammed his fist down on the hard surface of his desk. He welcomed the pain. Damned stubborn woman. Didn't she realize how unbalanced Kelvin was?

Well, no. She didn't. How could she when she'd never even met the man?

Lucas felt more confused than he'd been in his entire life. Perhaps he had overreacted. Maybe Kelvin was no threat to Corrie. He didn't even know her. On the other hand, if she was walking into danger, it was because of Lucas, because Kelvin had guessed she meant something to a Sinclair.

He tried to tell himself he was being foolish. He should have a little faith in Corrie. He'd already accepted that in order to take their relationship forward, they'd have to agree to disagree on some things. Compromise.

But not on this. Irrational as it seemed, he was convinced Corrie needed him at her side when she talked to Stanley Kelvin.

He glanced toward the file cabinet, where Corrie had claimed she'd seen the shade of Adrienne Sinclair. No woman in late-nineteenth-century dress stood there. But there was an odd shimmer in the air.

He blinked and it was gone, but he couldn't shake

the feeling that he'd just gotten the go-ahead from beyond the grave.

Stopping only to grab a coat, he left the Sinclair House at a run. Seconds later, squealing tires marked his exit from the hotel parking lot. He broke every speed limit in Waycross Springs, intent on getting to the Phoenix Inn in record time. He figured that if the cops chased him, so much the better.

TWELVE

Although she'd known that the Phoenix Inn was no longer on a par with the Sinclair House, Corrie was still shocked to walk in and see its run-down condition. While not precisely dirty, since that would have led to complaints of health and safety violations, the lobby was decorated with threadbare carpeting, poor-quality furniture and cheap reproductions of famous paintings.

The combined smells of stale tobacco, cheap whiskey, and spilled beer nearly overwhelmed her the moment she set foot inside. One end of the spacious reception area had been turned into a barroom.

"Yeah?" said the slovenly woman behind the registration desk.

"I have an appointment with Mr. Kelvin."

Snapping a wad of gum, the woman picked up an old-fashioned, rotary-dial black phone and slowly gave one number a turn. "Someone here to see you, *Mr.*

Kelvin." A nasal laugh accompanied the announcement. She hung up after a moment and sneered at Corrie. "He'll be out in a sec, honey. Sit yourself down and wait, why don't ya?"

Corrie considered telling the woman that she wouldn't dare sit on the furniture but decided there was no point in antagonizing her. Instead she wandered around the lobby, keeping as far away from the barroom end as she could.

It was impossible not to make comparisons. Like the Sinclair House, Stanley Kelvin's place possessed the stately lines and sweeping curves of grand hotel architecture, but with the effects of decades of neglect and decay it reminded her more of the seedy dumps portrayed in film noir movies of the thirties and forties. She half expected to see a Humphrey Bogart or James Cagney clone emerge from the door marked office.

Instead she got Stanley Kelvin.

"Come in. Come in." He actually rubbed his hands together in anticipation.

Corrie swallowed hard, wondering if she knew what she was doing after all.

Where Lucas had kept the furniture of the last century for his office—that massive oak desk, the antique file cabinet, and a deep, beautifully colored Persian carpet—Stanley Kelvin had installed two rickety chairs, a cheap, unfinished kneehole desk, the kind that came in a box labeled "some assembly required," and a gunmetal-gray file cabinet that appeared to be army surplus.

"It wasn't always like this," he said defensively.

"I'm sorry. I didn't mean to—"

But he wasn't interested in hearing her apology. Kelvin was still talking. "I only just got it back from the guy who bought it when I declared bankruptcy. I'll fix it up. You wait and see. After the Sinclairs go out of business, the customers will flock here in droves."

Appalled, Corrie kept silent. He actually believed what he was saying. Suddenly she felt sorry for him.

She also wished she hadn't come. Could she reveal only that she was descended from the missing Marguerite and not the secret of Jonathan's questionable birth without letting Adrienne down? She hoped so, because she didn't have it in her to shatter the dreams of this poor excuse for a man. Dreams were probably all he had.

"Well? What do you want to know about the Sinclairs?" he asked her.

"Actually I've come here under false pretenses," she confessed nervously. "There's something I want to tell you. It's about a woman named Marguerite Mead."

Before she could explain that Marguerite Mead and her own great-grandmother, Daisy, were one and the same, Kelvin seized her by the shoulders. His fingers pinched her and she cried out.

"Son of a bitch," he swore.

With genuine confusion, and the beginning of real fear, Corrie gaped at the snarling little man. Stanley Kelvin was far stronger than he looked. He all but dragged her across his office into a smaller attached room.

"Now, wait just a minute—"

"Shut up. Let me think." He released her but stood so that he blocked the exit.

Corrie subsided, watching him warily. They were in some sort of storage closet, a windowless, empty room from which there was no obvious means of escape.

Don't argue with him, she warned herself. Desperately, she tried to think of some way out of this situation. She wished now that she'd asked Lucas to come with her. She'd been much too quick to dismiss his warnings about Stanley Kelvin.

Standing in Kelvin's office, hidden by the shadow of the door, Lucas barely restrained the urge to rush to the rescue, but he could see Corrie. She was unhurt. And although he'd arrived in time to see the momentary panic Kelvin's actions had roused in her, now she seemed to be coping.

"Let me tell you about the Meads and the Sinclairs," Kelvin was muttering. "The Meads may have done some terrible things, but the Sinclairs are every bit as wicked."

"I'd like to hear what you have to say," Corrie said. Her voice shook a little, but she sounded sincere. "However, I think you've misunderstood my reason for being here."

"I was just a boy," Kelvin whined, paying no attention to Corrie's words at all. "My mother was a widow. Hugh Sinclair thought that meant she was fair game."

Suddenly Lucas wanted to hear whatever Kelvin had to say too.

"He never intended to marry her. He didn't want to be saddled with raising another man's son."

Stanley Kelvin's father, Lucas recalled, had been killed during World War II. Hugh hadn't been old enough to enlist. That meant he'd been barely twenty during the time Kelvin was babbling about. Maybe a young man sowing wild oats but hardly a seasoned seducer. If he'd been intimate with Kelvin's mother, an older woman, it had to have been at Rita Kelvin's invitation.

That wasn't an image Lucas cared for. He remembered "old lady" Kelvin as the woman who called the cops every time a bunch of kids took a shortcut across her backyard.

"He ruined her life," Kelvin complained. He was pacing, ignoring Corrie completely. "He ruined mine too. She loved him and he abandoned her. Left town. Came back married to another woman."

A quick calculation reassured Lucas. What Kelvin tried to make seem like a matter of months had actually been some fifteen years.

Hugh had been thirty-five when he'd met and married Lucas's mother.

"I'm sorry for that," Corrie said, "but it wasn't the Marguerite who was your mother that I wanted to talk about. It was the earlier one. Horatio Mead's runaway daughter."

"Oh, I know about her too." Bitterness made Kelvin's voice harsh, but there was a slight relaxation in the set of his shoulders. Lucas wondered what had prompted his sudden prickly defense of his mother, then decided he didn't want to go down that road, not even in his imagination.

"What do you mean?" Corrie asked Kelvin.

"She abandoned her family. Betrayed the Meads. Just as the sainted Adrienne did. Marguerite was supposed to marry old Nehemiah Jones, so he'd invest in the hotel. She ran off with the local bootmaker instead."

"Mr. Skinner," Corrie murmured. She'd begun to edge toward the door.

"Hold it right there," Kelvin ordered. "I don't trust you."

"The feeling is mutual, Mr. Kelvin. Why are we here in this . . . closet? Wouldn't it be pleasanter to discuss our business in the lobby? Let me buy you a drink."

His laugh was nasty. "I wouldn't touch the rotgut they serve at my bar."

"Then I think I'd better be leaving." Corrie's voice shook, enough to prompt Lucas to take action.

Before Kelvin could even think about making any threatening moves, Lucas had pushed past him to shield Corrie with his own body. The expression of relieved surprise on her face set his heart racing. He'd been concerned she'd resent his interference.

"Time to leave now?" he suggested.

She seemed to get her nerve back once she knew

she was not alone, and said, "Perhaps a moment more?"

Kelvin might be wary of Lucas's greater physical strength, but he plastered on his familiar smirk. "If you're going to tell me you want to go looking for Marguerite's heirs," he told Corrie, "I can assure you that you'll be wasting your time. I lost this place to bankruptcy. Then I bought it back with my own hard-earned money. It's really mine now. Nothing can take it from me."

Bought with money embezzled from the Sinclairs? Lucas wondered. In spite of that suspicion, he couldn't help feeling sorry for Stanley Kelvin. This pathetic man had plainly grown up under the thumb of a twisted and vindictive mother who'd taught him to hate because her own desires had been thwarted.

"I am Marguerite's heir," Corrie said, "but I don't want your hotel. I only want what Adrienne Sinclair must have wanted, for both families to know and accept the truth."

"We've always known." Kelvin looked insufferably smug. "Old Jonathan hated his sister. Horatio sent him to find her. Jonathan came back and told the old man she was dead. End of story."

"Not quite."

Lucas was concerned about how much more Corrie meant to tell Kelvin, but he didn't try to stop her.

"The rest of my family needs to be told," she said. "And the Sinclairs."

Kelvin shrugged. "So tell them."

Lucas waited.

After a moment, Corrie nodded. "End of story," she said. "And it had better be the end of the feud as well." She looked Stanley Kelvin right in the eye. "One more hint of trouble at the Sinclair House and I go straight to Officer Tandy and report that you assaulted me."

Kelvin sputtered in protest, but she cut him off.

"With your record, who do you think a jury will believe? Smarten up, Mr. Kelvin. You stay in your hotel and we'll stay in ours."

Grinning broadly, Lucas offered Corrie his arm. When she took it, they swept out of the closet and through the office in a grand manner that would have made Adrienne proud. Neither of them spoke until they were safely inside Corrie's car and heading back across town. Lucas left the hotel van behind to be picked up later.

"You were right," she said. "I shouldn't have gone alone."

"I should have offered to go with you."

He could feel her intense gaze on his profile as he drove. "You do realize I'm *related* to that man? That he's *family*?" she asked.

"I don't recommend that you embrace Kelvin as a cousin. Look what happened to Pop when he tried."

"Don't worry about it." She paused. "Do you suppose I convinced him to end the feud?"

"You convinced me. I especially liked the way you referred to the Sinclair House as *our* hotel."

He glanced her way and wondered why the inside of the car hadn't caught on fire. The look in her eyes raised his internal temperature to a boil and turned his voice raspy. They might have been talking about Kelvin, but she sure as hell wasn't thinking about any man but Lucas.

"I intend to embrace *my* newfound cousin," he vowed. "Often."

"You mean me?" she whispered.

"I mean you." With an effort, he forced himself to pay attention to his driving. Keeping his eyes on the road ahead cleared his mind enough to warn him to be sensible. He mustn't rush Corrie. They had all the time in the world now.

"Ready to share this story with my folks and your father?" he asked.

"Do we have a last chapter yet?"

He thought about that for a moment. "Not yet," he conceded, "but I'm convinced you and I are headed for a happy ending." He dared another quick glance. Again she was watching him intently. "I know we need to take it slow. Get to know each other better without matchmakers or ghosts involved. But I can't help believing we have . . . something ahead of us."

Her voice sounded as breathless as he felt. "Yes," she said. "Definitely . . . something."

A short time later, at Lucas's parents' house, Corrie told the story of what she'd discovered one more time, revealing the reason Adrienne had come back to haunt the Sinclair House and her own connection to the family.

She felt a growing sense of belonging there. And an inexplicable but very strong certainty that Lucas had stopped doubting her. Impossible or not, he accepted that she'd been in contact with Adrienne's spirit.

A sudden movement from Hugh startled them all. Slowly, laboriously, he rolled his wheelchair to the desk and began to type a message into the laptop. Lucas went to stand behind him, reading over his shoulder.

"According to Pop," he said after a few minutes, "the Todds came here to visit because Corrie's grandmother, Alice Todd's mother, had always talked about the place. They didn't know of her connection to the family. Or if they did, they never mentioned it to Pop or his father. They arrived late in the day and were disappointed to find the hotel closed for the season."

"But somehow they got in." Corrie had been watching Hugh and was relieved to observe that he did not seem upset. He wanted to tell his story.

Lucas nodded. "My grandfather, Pop's father, was a generous man. He felt sorry for Mrs. Todd, so, on an impulse, he invited them to stay anyway. Pop was annoyed about that. First, because they were already worried about the wildfires. They didn't need guests to look out for. Then because the daughter claimed she'd seen a ghost."

"She wanted to stay longer," Corrie guessed.

"Yes. Pitched a fit when she was told they had to leave. That was the quarrel you saw, Corrie. And it took place when Pop insisted they evacuate because of the fire danger."

"And the claim that she'd seen a ghost? He did nothing about that?"

"He had other things to worry about at the time."

"The hotel lost one wing to the flames," Joyce reminded her.

Lucas nodded. "That was the very next day. Pop says he did wonder, but the Todds let the matter drop. They never came back. He figured the girl just had an overactive imagination. He never gave the incident another thought until you came along, Corrie. Your experiences stirred up the old memory, and a sense of guilt because he hadn't pursued it."

"And that's all Adrienne wanted to convey?" Donald Ballantyne asked. "That Marguerite was the real heir because Jonathan Mead was the love child of Cordelia La Fleur and some unknown man?"

"Oh, not unknown," Joyce said. "It's quite obvious who he was."

Everyone turned to look at her, even Hugh.

"Well, to be more accurate, I can make an educated guess from studying old family photographs." She trotted over to the bookshelves and withdrew one of her albums. When she found the page she wanted, she held the book out to Corrie. "There. See? That's Douglas Sinclair, the older brother of the first Lucas. He left the area sometime around 1875 to go out West with his wife and family. Never came back."

Douglas had not been on the family tree Joyce had given her.

"You're saying Douglas was Jonathan's father?" Lucas asked. "That Jonathan was a *Sinclair*?" He sounded appalled, and Corrie could guess why. This put Kelvin back in the family again.

Joyce flipped through the album until she found another photograph and extracted it to show around side by side with the portrait of Douglas. "Here's Jonathan's picture. You see? You can hardly miss the resemblance."

They were as alike as Hugh and Lucas.

"Do you think Horatio knew?" Corrie asked.

"Who can tell? Once he married Cordelia, though, he accepted her son as his own. Then, of course, they had Marguerite. It's possible Jonathan suspected who his real father was. He certainly had some problem with self-esteem. Everything I've read about him in old records indicates he wasn't a very pleasant man. Petty. Quarrelsome. It didn't surprise me to hear he lied to old Horatio, telling him Marguerite was dead so he'd have exclusive claim to the Phoenix Inn."

"This is way too complicated for me," Corrie's father said. "Why go to all that bother?"

"Horatio might well have disowned Jonathan if Adrienne had told him Marguerite was still alive," Corrie explained. "Even if she didn't force him to acknowledge the truth of Jonathan's paternity, there would still be the fact that Jonathan had lied about Marguerite being dead." Horatio had loved his daughter. Corrie had seen that for herself the day he burst into the dining room at the Sinclair House.

Joyce was nodding. "That Adrienne didn't speak

up before she died must have been what kept her from resting in peace. It may not seem like much to us today, but back then it would have been a very big deal."

"Do you suppose we'll ever know if this is the right solution?" Lucas wondered.

"Oh, I think so." Corrie sent Lucas a smile meant just for him. "If it isn't, we'll be seeing Adrienne again."

The only one around with a stronger sense of family, she mused, was Adrienne Sinclair's great-great-grandson.

Four months later, Corrie's wedding day dawned clear and bright, a perfect May morning. It was the warmest spring on record, too, to everyone's great relief. She spent a few minutes going over the final plans for the following week's Cozies Unlimited conference at the hotel, part of her job now that she was in charge of PR for the Sinclair House, then went to the armoire to take out her wedding gown.

Rachel came breezing in, holding up a delicate lace garter. "I've got your something borrowed."

"Are you sure that isn't the something old?"

Her something blue was a bouquet that contained the first forget-me-nots of spring, chosen to match her eyes, Lucas said.

"Could be both. It came out of a trunk in Joyce's attic. I'm betting it belonged to the first Mrs. Lucas Sinclair."

Adrienne.

No one had seen the ghost or experienced any sense of her presence since Corrie's last dream. She hoped that meant she had succeeded in righting all the old wrongs, as much as they could be righted after the passage of so much time. Still, Corrie could not help wishing for some sign that Adrienne approved of what she'd done.

She took the garter from Rachel and began to dress.

A short time later, she stepped out of the hotel on her father's arm and started down the path that led to the man-made pond. Donald nodded his gruff approval and kissed her on the cheek. "Your mother would be proud of you," he said.

As they moved past the grove of trees, a small orchestra struck up Purcell's "Trumpet Voluntary." Corrie felt as if she were floating toward the gathered guests.

Rachel, as maid of honor, led the way along the flagstones toward waiting family and friends. So much family, Corrie thought. Even her brother's Saint Bernard was in attendance, well-behaved for once and sitting next to her nephews.

The only family member missing was a distant cousin named Stanley Kelvin. She didn't regret his absence. The truce seemed to be holding as he slowly built up his own business and left the Sinclair House alone.

Then Corrie caught sight of Lucas, waiting for her at the flower-covered bower with the minister, and all thoughts of other people vanished. Their gazes locked. She moved to his side.

They had written the words themselves, promises of a lifetime of love and devotion to each other. The ceremony had a dreamlike quality, yet nothing had ever felt so real. As Lucas pledged himself to her and she murmured her vows in return, Corrie knew she had never in her life done anything more right or been happier.

They kissed and then, still holding hands, turned to face their well-wishers.

"Enjoy already," Rachel whispered.

But Corrie barely heard her best friend.

There, just at the entrance to the grove, another couple stood hand in hand, beatific smiles on their shimmering faces. "Lucas?" she breathed.

"I see them."

As Corrie and Lucas watched, the shades of Adrienne and her Lucas grew fainter and fainter and finally faded away entirely. Corrie felt no sadness at this last glimpse of the ghost who'd changed her life. She and her Lucas were reunited at last.

"Till death do us part," Corrie's Lucas whispered, "and beyond."

"Happily ever after," she pledged, "and happily ever *here*after too."

THE EDITORS' CORNER

As the year draws to a close, we're delighted to bring you some Christmas cheer to warm and gladden your hearts. December's LOVESWEPTs will put a smile on your face and love on your mind, and when you turn that last page, you'll sigh longingly and maybe even wipe a few stray tears off your cheeks.

Rachel Lawrence and Sam Wyatt are setting off **FIREWORKS** in LOVESWEPT #862 by rising star RaeAnne Thayne. The last time Rachel left Whiskey Creek, she swore she'd never return. The only two people in the world who can force her to break her vow are her nephews. The problem is, Rachel and their father, Sam, can't stand each other. Now that Rachel's back in town, the sparks are flying. Sam can't understand why Rachel would take such a vested interest in the welfare of his sons—he just wants her to leave before he acts on the desire he feels for her. Rachel fears giving in to feelings for Sam she's harbored in her heart, harbored even before she lost her young husband in a brushfire. But when another brushfire threatens to claim the family ranch, will she forgive Sam for choosing duty over love? RaeAnne Thayne's tale sizzles with passion and is sure to keep you warm on even the coldest winter night!

In LOVESWEPT #863, Laura Taylor delivers **THE CHRISTMAS GIFT.** Former attorney Jack Howell thought his toughest cases were behind him, but when he returns to Kentucky to explore his new-found roots, he faces his most baffling case of all—an infant boy abandoned on his doorstep. Interior decorator Chloe McNeil's temper starts to simmer when Jack doesn't keep their appointment to discuss his new home. Maybe she's misjudged this man who so easily found a way into her heart. But when she drops by to give him a piece of her mind, she finds him knee-deep in diapers and formula. As Jack and Chloe care for the baby and try to keep Social Services from taking him away, will they discover that cherishing this child together is just the healing magic they need? Well-loved author Laura Taylor unites two wounded spirits during the season of Christmas harmony.

Remember Candy Johnson, Jen Casey's best friend in FOR LOVE OR MONEY, LOVESWEPT #849? Well, she's back with a hunk of her own in Kathy DiSanto's **HUNTER IN DISGUISE,** LOVESWEPT #864. Candy is sure there's more to George Price than his chunky glasses and ever-present pocket protector. For example, a chest and tush of Greek-god standards. And why would a gym teacher take out the soccer balls for the girls vs. guys volleyball match? And let's not forget about his penchant for B 'n' E (breaking and entering, that is). In the meantime, George has a problem all his own—trying to distract armchair detective Candy long enough to get his job done. George's less-than-debonair attributes prove to be easy enough to ignore as Candy gets to know the man beneath the look. Kathy DiSanto spins a breathless tale that's part wicked romp, part sexy suspense, and all pure pleasure!

Please welcome newcomer Catherine Mulvany to our Loveswept family as she presents **UPON A MIDNIGHT CLEAR**, LOVESWEPT #865. Alexandra Roundtree's obituary clearly stated she was no longer one of Brunswick, Oregon's, living citizens, but private investigator Dixon Yano is disabused of that notion when she comes walking into his agency in full disguise. Alex pleads with Dixon to help her find her would-be murderer, and after shots are fired through his window, Dixon decides to be her bodyguard. Soon, Dixon and Alex are forced into close quarters and intimate encounters. Even after her last romantic fiasco, Alex finds herself trusting in the man who has become her swashbuckling hero and lifesaver. Will Dixon cross the line between business and pleasure if it means risking his lady's life? Catherine Mulvany's first novel mixes up an explosively sensual cocktail that will touch and tantalize the soul!

Happy reading!

With warmest wishes,

Susann Brailey

Joy Abella

Susann Brailey
Senior Editor

Joy Abella
Administrative Editor

P.S. Look for these Bantam women's fiction titles coming in December! *New York Times* bestseller Iris Johansen is back with **LONG AFTER MIDNIGHT,** now available in paperback. Research scientist Kate Denham mistakenly believes she's finally carved out a secure life for herself and her son, only to be thrown suddenly into a nightmare world where danger is all around and trusting a handsome stranger is the only way to survive. Hailed as "a queen of erotic, exciting romance," Susan Johnson gives us **TABOO.** Andre Duras and Teo Korsakova are thrown together during the chaotic times of the Napoleonic Wars, igniting a glorious passion even as conflicting loyalties threaten to tear them apart. And finally, a charmer from the gifted Michelle Martin—**STOLEN MOMENTS**—a stylish contemporary romance about the man hired to track down a beautiful young pop singer who is tired of fame and has decided to explore Manhattan incognito. And immediately following this page, preview the Bantam women's fiction titles on sale in October!

For current information on Bantam's women's fiction, visit our Web site, *Isn't It Romantic,* at the following address: **http://www.bdd.com/romance**

Don't miss these extraordinary books
by your favorite Bantam authors!

On sale in October:

FINDING LAURA
by Kay Hooper

HAWK O'TOOLE'S HOSTAGE
by Sandra Brown

IT HAPPENED ONE NIGHT
by Leslie LaFoy

"Kay Hooper is a multitalented author whose stories always pack a tremendous punch."
—Iris Johansen, *New York Times* bestselling author of *The Ugly Duckling*

POWER AND MONEY ARE
NO PROTECTION FROM FATE—
OR MURDER. . . .

FINDING LAURA
by Kay Hooper

Over the years, the wealthy, aloof Kilbourne family has suffered a number of suspicious deaths. Now the charming, seductive Peter Kilbourne has been found stabbed to death in a seedy motel room. And for Laura Sutherland, a struggling artist, nothing will ever be the same. Because she was one of the last people to see him alive—and one of the first to be suspected of his murder.

Now, determined to clear her name and uncover the truth about the murder—and the antique mirror that had recently brought Peter into her life—Laura will breach the iron gates of the Kilbourne estate . . . only to find that every Kilbourne, from the enigmatic Daniel to the steely matriarch Amelia to Peter's disfigured widow, Kerry, has something to hide. But which one of them looks in the mirror and sees the reflection of a killer? And which one will choose Laura to be the next to die?

"Miss Sutherland? I'm Peter Kilbourne."

A voice to break hearts.

Laura gathered her wits and stepped back, opening the door wider to admit him. "Come in." She thought he was about her own age, maybe a year or two older.

He came into the apartment and into the living room, taking in his surroundings quickly but thoroughly, and clearly taking note of the mirror on the coffee table. His gaze might have widened a bit when it fell on her collection of mirrors, but Laura couldn't be sure, and when he turned to face her, he was smiling with every ounce of his charm.

It was unsettling how instantly and powerfully she was affected by that magnetism. Laura had never considered herself vulnerable to charming men, but she knew without doubt that this one would be difficult to resist—whatever it was he wanted of her. Too uneasy to sit down or invite him to, Laura merely stood with one hand on the back of a chair and eyed him with what she hoped was a faint, polite smile.

If Peter Kilbourne thought she was being ungracious in not inviting him to sit down, he didn't show it. He gestured slightly toward the coffee table and said, "I see you've been hard at work, Miss Sutherland."

She managed a shrug. "It was badly tarnished. I wanted to get a better look at the pattern."

He nodded, his gaze tracking past her briefly to once again note the collection of mirrors near the hallway. "You have quite a collection. Have you . . . always collected mirrors?"

It struck her as an odd question somehow, perhaps because there was something hesitant in his tone, something a bit surprised in his eyes. But Laura replied truthfully despite another stab of uneasiness. "Since I was a child, actually. So you can see why I bought that one today at the auction."

"Yes." He slid his hands into the pockets of his dark slacks, sweeping open his suit jacket as he did so in a pose that might have been studied or merely relaxed. "Miss Sutherland—look, do you mind if I call you Laura?"

"No, of course not."

"Thank you," he nodded gravely, a faint glint of amusement in his eyes recognizing her reluctance. "I'm Peter."

She nodded in turn, but didn't speak.

"Laura, would you be interested in selling the mirror back to me? At a profit, naturally."

"I'm sorry." She was shaking her head even before he finished speaking. "I don't want to sell the mirror."

"I'll give you a hundred for it."

Laura blinked in surprise, but again shook her head. "I'm not interested in making money, Mr. Kilbourne—"

"Peter."

A little impatiently, she said, "All right—Peter. I don't want to sell the mirror. And I did buy it legitimately."

"No one's saying you didn't, Laura," he soothed. "And you aren't to blame for my mistake, certainly. Look, the truth is that the mirror shouldn't have been put up for auction. It's been in my family a long time, and we'd like to have it back. Five hundred."

Not a bad profit on a five-dollar purchase. She drew a breath and spoke slowly. "No. I'm sorry, I really am, but . . . I've been looking for this—for a mirror like this—for a long time. To add to my collection. I'm not interested in making money, so please don't bother to raise your offer. Even five thousand wouldn't make a difference."

His eyes were narrowed slightly, very intent on her face, and when he smiled suddenly it was with rueful certainty. "Yes, I can see that. You don't have to look so uneasy, Laura—I'm not going to wrest the thing away from you by force."

"I never thought you would," she murmured, lying.

He chuckled, a rich sound that stroked along her nerve endings like a caress. "No? I'm afraid I've made you nervous, and that was never my intention. Why don't I buy you dinner some night as an apology?"

This man is dangerous. "That isn't necessary," she said.

"I insist."

Laura looked at his incredibly handsome face, that charming smile, and drew yet another deep breath. "Will your wife be coming along?" she asked mildly.

"If she's in town, certainly." His eyes were guileless.

Very dangerous. Laura shook her head. "Thanks, but no apology is necessary. You offered a generous price for the mirror; I refused. That's all there is to it." She half turned and made a little gesture toward the door with one hand, unmistakably inviting him to leave.

Peter's beautiful mouth twisted a bit, but he obeyed the gesture and followed her to the door. When she opened it and stood back, he paused to reach into the inner pocket of his jacket and produced a business card. "Call me if you change your mind," he said. "About the mirror, I mean."

Or anything else, his smile said.

"I'll do that," she returned politely, accepting the card.

"It was nice meeting you, Laura."

"Thank you. Nice meeting you," she murmured.

He gave her a last flashing smile, lifted a hand slightly in a small salute, and left her apartment.

Laura closed the door and leaned back against it for a moment, relieved and yet still uneasy. She didn't know why Peter Kilbourne wanted the mirror back badly enough to pay hundreds of dollars for it, but every instinct told her the matter was far from settled.

She hadn't heard the last of him.

Her novels are sensual and moving, compelling and richly satisfying. That's why *New York Times* bestselling phenomenon **Sandra Brown** is one of America's best-loved romance writers. Now, the passionate struggle between a modern-day outlaw and his feisty, beautiful captive erupts in

HAWK O'TOOLE'S HOSTAGE

To Hawk O'Toole, she was a pawn in a desperate gamble to help his people. To Miranda Price, he was a stranger who'd done the unthinkable: kidnapped her and her young son off a train full of sight-seeing vacationers. Now, held hostage on a distant reservation for reasons she cannot at first fathom, Miranda finds herself battling a captor who is by turns harsh and tender, mysteriously aloof and dangerously seductive.

"You know me?" She tried not to reveal her anxiety through her voice.

"I know who you are."

"Then you have me at a distinct disadvantage."

"That's right. I do."

She had hoped to weasel out his name, but he lapsed into stoic silence as the horse carefully picked its way down the steep incline. As hazardous as the race up the mountainside had been, traveling down the other side was more so. Miranda expected the horse's forelegs to buckle at any second and pitch them forward. They wouldn't stop rolling until they hit bottom several miles below. She was afraid for

Scott. He was still crying, though not hysterically as before.

"That man my son is riding with, does he know how to ride well?"

"Ernie was practically born on a horse. He won't let anything happen to the boy. He's got several sons of his own."

"Then he must understand how I feel!" she cried.

When she reflexively laid her hand on his thigh, she inadvertently touched his holster. The pistol was within her grasp! All she had to do was play it cool. If she could catch him off guard, she had a chance of whipping the pistol out of the holster and turning it on him. She could stave off the others while holding their leader at gunpoint long enough for Scott to get on the horse with her. Surely she could find her way back to the train where law enforcement agencies must already be organizing search parties. Their trail wouldn't be difficult to follow, for no efforts had been taken to cover it. They could still be found well before dark.

But in the meantime, she had to convince the outlaw that she was resigned to her plight and acquiescent to his will. Gradually, so as not to appear obvious, she let her body become more pliant against his chest. She ceased trying to maintain space between her thighs and his. She no longer kept her hip muscles contracted, but let them go soft against his lap, which grew perceptibly tighter and harder with each rocking motion of the saddle.

Eventually her head dropped backward onto his shoulder, as though she had dozed off. She made certain he could see that her eyes were closed. She knew he was looking down at her because she could feel his breath on her face and the side of her neck. Taking a deep breath, she intentionally lifted her breasts high, until they strained against her lightweight summer blouse. When they settled, they settled heavily on the arm he still held across her midriff.

But she didn't dare move her hand, not until she thought the moment was right. By then her heart had begun to pound so hard she was afraid he might feel it against his arm. Sweat had moistened her palms. She hoped her hand wouldn't be too slippery to grab the butt of the pistol. To avoid that, she knew she must act without further delay.

In one motion, she sat up straight and reached for the pistol.

He reacted quicker.

His fingers closed around her wrist like a vise and prized her hand off the gun. She grunted in pain and gave an anguished cry of defeat and frustration.

"Mommy?" Scott shouted from up ahead. "Mommy, what's the matter?"

Her teeth were clenched against the pain the outlaw was inflicting on the fragile bones of her wrist, but she managed to choke out, "Nothing, darling. Nothing. I'm fine." Her captor's grip relaxed, and she called to Scott, "How are you?"

"I'm thirsty and I have to go to the bathroom."

"Tell him it's not much farther."

She repeated the dictated message to her son. For the time being Scott seemed satisfied. Her captor let the others go on ahead until the last horse was almost out of sight before he placed one hand beneath her jaw and jerked her head around to face him.

"If you want to handle something hard and deadly, Mrs. Price, I'll be glad to direct your hand to something just as steely and fully loaded as the pistol. But then you already know how hard it is, don't you?

You've been grinding your soft little tush against it for the last twenty minutes." His eyes darkened. "Don't underestimate me again."

The situation had taken on a surreal aspect.

That was dispelled the moment the man dismounted and pulled her down to stand beside him. After the lengthy horseback ride, her thighs quivered under the effort of supporting her. Her feet were numb. Before she regained feeling in them, Scott hurled his small body at her shins and closed his arms around her thighs, burying his face in her lap.

She dropped to her knees in front of him and embraced him tightly, letting tears of relief roll down her cheeks. They had come this far and had escaped serious injury. She was grateful for that much. After a lengthy bear hug, she held Scott away from her and examined him. He seemed none the worse for wear, except for his eyes, which were red and puffy from crying. She drew him to her chest again and hugged him hard.

Too soon, a long shadow fell across them. Miranda looked up. Their kidnapper had taken off the white duster, his gloves, his gun belt, and his hat. His straight hair was as inky black as the darkness surrounding them. The firelight cast wavering shadows across his face that blunted its sharp angles but made it appear more sinister.

That didn't deter Scott. Before Miranda realized what he was going to do, the child flung himself against the man. He kicked at the long shins with his tennis shoes and pounded the hard, lean thighs with his grubby fists.

"You hurt my mommy. I'm gonna beat you up. You're a bad man. I hate you. I'm gonna kill you. You leave my mommy alone."

His high, piping voice filled the still night air. Miranda reached out to pull Scott back, but the man held up his hand to forestall her. He endured Scott's ineffectual attack until the child's strength had been spent and the boy collapsed into another torrent of tears.

The man took the boy's shoulders between his hands. "You are very brave."

His low, resonant voice calmed Scott instantly. With solemn, tear-flooded eyes, Scott gazed up at the man. "Huh?"

"You are very brave to go up against an enemy so much stronger than yourself." The others in the outlaw band had clustered around them, but the boy had the man's attention. He squatted down, putting himself on eye level with Scott. "It's also a fine thing for a man to defend his mother the way you just did." From a scabbard attached to his belt, he withdrew a knife. Its blade was short, but sufficient. Miranda drew in a quick breath. The man tossed the knife into the air. It turned end over end until he deftly caught it by the tip of the blade. He extended the ivory handle toward Scott.

"Keep this with you. If I ever hurt your mother, you can stab me in the heart with it."

Wearing a serious expression, Scott took the knife. Ordinarily, accepting a gift from a stranger would have warranted parental permission. Scott, his eyes fixed on the man before him, didn't even glance at Miranda. For the second time that afternoon, her son had obeyed this man without consulting her first. That, almost as much as their perilous situation, bothered her.

"Hmm. Can I go to the bathroom now?"

"There is no bathroom here. The best we can offer is the woods."

"That's okay. Sometimes Mommy lets me go outside if we're on picnics and stuff." He sounded agreeable enough, but he glanced warily at the wall of darkness beyond the glow of the campfire.

"Ernie will go with you," Hawk reassured him, pressing his shoulder as he stood up. "When you come back, he'll get you something to drink."

"Okay. I'm kinda hungry, too."

Ernie stepped forward and extended his hand to the boy, who took it without hesitation. They turned and, with the other men, headed toward the campfire. Miranda made to follow. The man named Hawk stepped in front of her and barred her path. "Where do you think you're going?"

"To keep an eye on my son."

"Your son will be fine without you."

"Get out of my way."

Instead, he clasped her upper arms and walked her backward until she came up against the rough bark of a pine tree. Hawk kept moving forward until his body was pinning hers against the tree trunk. The brilliant blue eyes moved over her face, down her neck, and across her chest.

"Your son seems to think you're worth fighting for." His head lowered, coming closer to hers. "Are you?"

IT HAPPENED
ONE NIGHT
by Leslie LaFoy

*Alanna Chapman knows that no accountant worth her salt
would leave town during tax season, but now she has no
choice. To honor her aunt's final wishes, the Colorado CPA
has come to the mist-shrouded shores of Ireland, intending
to stay just long enough to accomplish her mission. But on
the mysterious grounds of Carraig Cor, something extraordinary happens: Alanna finds herself catapulted back to the
year 1803. Taken for a "seer" who can foretell Ireland's
future, she becomes the prisoner of a ruthless privateer . . . a dangerously attractive sea captain who has no
doubt that he can bend this modern temptress to his will, to
use her magic powers for his own ends. But when Alanna
crossed over to the nineteenth century, she didn't leave her
independent spirit behind. Now she's looking for a way to
escape the captain's irresistible embrace—and his enemy's
notice—before this perilous adventure costs her her
heart . . . and her life.*

Alanna raced to the door of the cabin, fighting back
panic and daring not a single look back. She knew
with absolute certainty that it wouldn't be long before
he staggered to his feet and came after her, that the
seconds between now and his vengeance were pre-

cious. The latch lifted and the door opened without resistance. Barefoot, with her hair streaming behind her, she fled down a dimly lit corridor toward a short flight of steep stairs. Hiking the gown above her knees, she clambered up the worn wooden steps, taking them two at a time. Her breath ragged and her heart pounding, she burst from the bowels of the ship onto the deck. Sliding to a sudden halt, Alanna glanced about the now clouded night, quickly noting the silent activity of shadowed male shapes and the world which lay beyond her floating prison. No light, of either man or heaven, sought to break the darkness. Her sight adjusted as she gazed to her left and out across the open sea. Turning to her right, she saw, beyond a wide expanse of green water, the rocky shoreline she had glimpsed from the window of Kiervan's cabin.

Ahead of her the ship narrowed to a long thick pole that stretched out over the sea. Alanna whirled about. The doorway from which she had emerged onto the deck sat in the center of a squat, flat-topped blockhouse. A few feet to her left another steep but short flight of stairs led upward. With relief, she noted that the structure didn't fill the entire width of the ship. On both sides, between it and the railings, a wide space permitted easy passage to the rear of the vessel. Pivoting to her right, Alanna dashed for the corner.

She was three-quarters of the way down the deck, with the unmistakable silhouette of a dinghy in sight, when a human shape stepped from around the corner and squarely into her path.

She stumbled to a halt. "Colleen, 'tis dangerous for ye to be topside, don't ye know? Where be Kiervan?"

Paddy. And he showed not the slightest signs of being inebriated. With a sigh of relief, Alanna moved toward him, keeping her voice low as she said, "He's a madman, Mr. O'Connell. He thinks it's 1803. He thinks he's some gun-running privateer."

"But for the first, 'tis all true, colleen. The lad's mind be far sounder than that of most men."

She froze and then managed to sputter, "It's 1997!"

He shook his head. " 'Twas before you climbed the Carraig Cor, to be sure. Least 'twas that time from which Maude promised to return to Erin. Now come along, colleen," he said, stepping forward and extending his hand, "an' I'll be a-seein' ye safely returned to Kiervan's cabin."

She stared at him, shaking her head and backing beyond his reach. "You're just as crazy as he is."

" 'Tis a long day ye've had, to be sure, an' 'twill be only a long rest which makes the edges of the world a wee bit smoother. 'Twill be easier for ye in the mornin'." He moved toward her again as he added, "Let's be about findin' Kiervan now."

Again Alanna shook her head. "I don't think so."

"Ye canna stay up here. My lads will do ye no harm, but Kiervan's have no respect for what ye are. And a British patrol could come upon us at any time. 'Tis not safe for ye to be remainin' topside."

She wasn't safe anywhere aboard this floating loony bin. Alanna glanced toward the rocky island in the distance. The impulse and the decision came in the same fraction of time. Without a word she spun about, grasped the railing, and vaulted over the side. In midair she righted herself and entered the water with knifelike precision.

On sale in November:

LONG AFTER MIDNIGHT
by *Iris Johansen*

TABOO
by *Susan Johnson*

STOLEN MOMENTS
by *Michelle Martin*